SPELL CHECK

HEDGEWITCH FOR HIRE – BOOK 10

CHRISTINE POPE

This is a work of fiction. Names, characters, places, and incidents are either the product of the author's imagination or are used fictitiously. Any resemblance to actual events, places, organizations, or persons, whether living or dead, is entirely coincidental.

SPELL CHECK

The Medicine Goes Down

"WE THINK THE CHILD'S MEDICINE IS interfering with your medicine," Raymond Standingbear said, his tone grave.

I blinked at him as he sat across the dining room table from Calvin and me. The two of us had invited Calvin's parents, Raymond and Delia, to dinner that lovely late September night, partly because it had been a while since we'd played host...but mostly because we wanted to talk in private about the little hiccup that had been a part of my life ever since I got pregnant back in June.

My ability to see auras had disappeared around then, and so far had given no indication that it ever intended to return. At first, I hadn't regarded their disappearance as anything more than a minor irritation, because they'd never been all that reliable, had come and gone as they pleased, and often weren't there when I needed them most—namely, when I was in the middle of one of my unofficial murder investigations and really could have used the extra insight they provided into a person's character.

But as the weeks and then months wore on, I realized that my talent for seeing auras appeared to have vanished for good. A decent span of time had passed before I even mentioned anything to Calvin, mostly because it didn't seem like the sort of thing I should be complaining about, not when everything else in my world seemed to be going along swimmingly. My pregnancy so far had been blessedly uneventful, and except for a couple of rocky weeks in the middle of my third month when pretty much any kind of food smell sent me bolting for the bathroom, I hadn't suffered any real side effects from being pregnant.

Well, except for my expanding waistline, of course. Even my beloved elastic-waist sequined skirts from India were getting a little tight, but luckily, the warm Arizona summers lasted well into fall in Globe, which meant I could get by with flowing maxi dresses and still not look as though I was wearing maternity clothes.

After I entered my fourth month, though, I'd confessed to Calvin that my ability to see auras appeared to have skated off to the Bahamas for the duration, and he'd told me we should consult with his parents.

"They know a lot more about supernatural stuff than I do," he'd said, a comment that had made me wrinkle my nose.

"I don't know if this exactly classifies as 'supernatural,'" I'd replied.

"Well, you're the only person I know who sees auras," he'd countered. "So it seems pretty supernatural to me."

That was true enough. And to be honest, the auras' disappearance had troubled me more than I wanted to acknowledge to myself. I might have used Tarot cards and pendulums to consult the universe and ask for its guidance, but the ability to see auras was my special gift, something I'd been born with...my own particular brand of magic. Having it suddenly gone made me feel as though a part of my essence was missing, as if I'd lost my sight or something.

And that was why Calvin and I now had the Standingbears sitting opposite us at the long dining room table in the house my husband and I shared. Even though it was the last of September, the air conditioning hummed quietly away in the background, keeping us cool on a day that had just barely missed hitting ninety a few hours earlier.

"'Medicine'?" I repeated. I hadn't made any

in-depth studies of Native American spiritual practices, but I knew enough to recall that the word had a very different meaning for the indigenous peoples of the United States, and sometimes referred to a person's spiritual power or energy.

"Yes," Delia said. Like her husband—and her son—she had night-black hair and eyes, and something of the sculpted beauty of her features was echoed in Calvin's face as well. "When Calvin told us what happened to your auras, Raymond and I discussed the problem, and we both agreed that seemed like the most logical explanation for what was going on."

"Because of who our people are?" Calvin asked, referring to the coyote-shifter nature of his tribe, the San Ramon Apaches. I'd only seen him change shape once, in a time before we were even together; it was a secret the San Ramon people had to hide from the rest of the world, for obvious reasons, and I knew I would carry their secret with me to the grave.

"That's what we believe," Delia replied. Her gaze flicked to me, concerned. "This is the first time any of the San Ramon Apache people have married an outsider or had children with them. None of us knew for sure what might happen."

True, we were all in uncharted waters here. My reassuringly ordinary pregnancy so far had seemed to indicate I didn't have to worry about giving birth to a coyote pup or something...even though Calvin had assured me that none of the children of his tribe showed that part of their natures until they were old enough to manage it...but those niggling worries remained, mostly because ours was a completely novel situation.

And honestly, if all I had to worry about was suppressed auras until the baby was born, I thought I could handle that.

"So...the child's magic is canceling out my magic?" I asked. I kind of hated to phrase it that way, because I still didn't think of my talent for seeing auras as exactly magic, but it seemed the simplest shortcut for the purposes of our current discussion.

"Possibly," Raymond said. "Or it may be the magic in the child is drawing your own magic toward him...or her. Again, we can't really be sure, since we've never encountered this kind of situation before."

I wasn't sure I liked the sound of that. Canceling out my magic was one thing, like the stronger flavor in a smoothie overpowering the other ingredients, but if the child was actually feeding off my magic, what did that mean? Was I carrying some kind of super-baby, some magically charged Chosen One or something?

As soon as the thought crossed my mind, I told myself to stop being ridiculous. Yes, with all those pregnancy hormones floating around in my system, I was probably more inclined than usual to leap to conclusions or let my emotions get the better of me, but that didn't mean I had to become a complete drama queen.

"So…what am I supposed to do about it?" I asked, knowing my tone sounded a little too plaintive. Beneath the table, Calvin's hand moved to take mine and give it a comforting squeeze.

Delia offered me a reassuring smile. Back when Calvin and I got together, she hadn't exactly been supportive of our relationship…to put it mildly…but now she was like a second mother to me, someone nearby who could offer me any encouragement or words of advice I might require. I loved my mom to death, but she was off in Southern California, hundreds of miles away, and couldn't be here to offer me the in-person support I needed. Yes, she'd promised to come stay for at least two or three weeks at their house in Globe with Tom, her husband, just as the baby was due to make an appearance, but that day was still many months off.

"Wait it out," Delia said. "True, we don't know exactly what we're dealing with here, but I have every reason to believe that as soon as the baby is born, your powers will return. Until then, you'll just have to do without."

On the surface, that suggestion seemed simple

enough. Because things had been quiet the past few months, ever since I'd proved my friend Archie's innocence in a particularly nasty murder case that occurred during one of the ballroom dance tournaments he and his fiancée Victoria had been participating in, I'd had no real reason to even need my aura-reading gift. Before I'd started solving murders, it had sometimes helped me out when I was trying to negotiate a contract, or even when I was deciding whether to take on a new client back when I was supporting myself with Tarot readings and other forms of spiritual guidance, but it wasn't anything that had been necessary in my day-to-day life.

Surely I could survive the next five and a half months without tapping into it, right?

Right.

"No problem," I said blithely, and reached for my glass of lemon-garnished San Pellegrino. Calvin sent me an oblique glance, one that told me he didn't consider the matter dropped, but to my relief, he didn't say anything.

For now, anyway.

As soon as the taillights of Raymond's Silverado had disappeared down the long gravel lane that led back to the main road, however, Calvin sent me a very direct look. "Are you sure you're okay with this?"

I didn't answer at first, and instead reached to pick up some of the glasses left behind on the table. Delia had insisted on clearing the plates and bowls from our dinner, but we'd lingered for a while after that, sipping our water, and so the drinkware still remained. "Well, I'm not sure whether it matters if I'm 'okay' with it or not. It is what it is."

His jaw tightened a little. Like me, he didn't have much use for that phrase, but sometimes it could be a little too appropriate for a given situation. "Maybe there's something we could do—"

"Like what?" I countered. "I have no idea where the auras came from in the first place, so it's not like I would even know where to begin when it comes to trying to get them back. About all I can do is hope that once the baby is here, they'll decide to return."

For a moment, he was silent, apparently considering my words. When he spoke, his tone was gentle. "You never really told me much about them."

No, I hadn't, because I'd taken the auras for granted, had thought they were as much a part of me as the color of my eyes or the annoying cowlick at my hairline that had convinced me I'd be much better off wearing bangs to conceal it.

"What's to say?" I said, my tone deliberately casual. "They started showing up when I was around thirteen. By then, I'd already started reading lots of books on witchcraft and psychics and the supernatural, so I knew what they were. They didn't frighten me or anything."

"No, I suppose they wouldn't have," Calvin replied, a faint smile touching those lips I loved so much. "You don't seem fazed by a whole lot."

I set the glasses I was carrying down on the counter next to the sink. "I don't?" I asked, my tone deliberately arch.

"No," he said, and came close so he could pull me into his arms and give me a much-needed kiss. He didn't taste like anything in particular, since we'd all been drinking lemon water, but his mouth was warm and welcome, exactly what I needed right then. "And what you're dealing with now… well, that's just a minor bump in the road."

"Exactly," I said, snuggling against his shoulder. "All I can do now is hope we don't have any murders I need to solve."

A reluctant chuckle sounded in my ear. "Considering your track record, that might be a little much to ask for."

True enough. Then again, we'd had an awfully long quiet span recently, all the way from the previous November to that unfortunate incident at the Stepping Stars tournament at the end of

May. If we had another murder-free stretch like that, then the baby would be safely here before I was required to put on my Sherlock Holmes hat again.

Fingers crossed.

Even as I sent that hope winging out into the universe, I couldn't quite quell the trickle of worry that went through me.

As I'd found all too often in the past, all the hopes and wishes in the world couldn't move the heavy hand of fate.

The Standingbears had come over on Saturday night, and the Sunday that followed was a quiet one, with both Calvin and me puttering around the house and taking care of whatever chores that had stacked up during the previous week. On Monday morning, I was back at my shop, Once in a Blue Moon, promptly at nine-thirty, ready to get a new week started. These days, I was flying solo, because Archie had opened his dance studio in the former antique store next door, and that meant I'd lost him as my assistant. Yes, I was happy he was now running his own business—and happier still that it looked as though it was going to be a success, something which hadn't been guaranteed in our small town of Globe—but the days felt a lot emptier now that I was back to working by myself.

True, sooner or later, I'd need to hire another assistant, someone I could train and have work with me for a few months before I had to go on a maternity leave whose length still hadn't been determined yet, but I hadn't quite taken the plunge and started formally advertising the position.

Oh, I'd asked around, made a few informal inquiries, but to my surprise, I had seen little interest so far. My friend Hazel had told me she'd pick up a shift or two if I needed to go to the doctor or run errands, but her career as an artist had been gaining momentum lately, so she didn't have a lot of time to spare, and definitely wasn't interested in being a full-time shop assistant.

And even though Globe didn't exactly have what you could call a thriving business district, it appeared everyone in our town was pretty set in their current professions and didn't see the need to make a change.

Which meant I'd probably have to put an ad on Craigslist or something and see if I could lure someone to my adopted hometown with the promise of a job that paid much better than minimum wage and also offered full benefits.

Luckily, I was able to do so, thanks to the money I'd inherited from Lucien Dumond, former head of the Greater Los Angeles Necromancers' Guild. It wasn't as though he and I had been close—far from it—but he'd decided he'd rather leave that money to me than to his murderous brother or any of his guild members. From time to time, I experienced a little guilt over having such a huge chunk of change dumped in my lap despite not doing anything to deserve it, although I did my best to assuage that guilt by being extremely generous with my charitable donations and doing whatever else I could to ensure I was spending the money on good deeds.

I'd just unlocked the front door and taken down the little "be back at" sign I hung in the window whenever the business was closed when Victoria Parrish, Archie's fiancée, came in the back entrance, which I'd already unlocked. We were now building-mates, since I'd gifted her my unused apartment upstairs, and she'd remodeled it into her design studio and office. However, lately she'd been so busy with the design of a new development currently under construction on the east side of town—she was doing all the interiors for the model homes—that I hadn't seen much of her for a couple of days.

"Just wanted to pop in and see when you can go in for your final fitting," she told me. "Can you do Wednesday at five-thirty?"

"Sure," I said, thinking it was thoughtful of

her to have scheduled the appointment after I was finished at the shop for the day. Yes, I could always hang up my trusty "be back at" sign and slip out in the middle of the afternoon if I had to, but this was much better.

"Perfect," she said. "Sorry I've been kind of scarce lately—the Mariposa Heights project is taking even more of my time than I thought it would."

"It's fine," I assured her. "I know you have a lot on your plate right now."

Which was probably the understatement of the year, since, besides overseeing the design of five different model homes, she was also in the final stages of planning her wedding with Archie. True, before she'd gotten her interior design certification, she'd been a highly successful wedding planner, and so she knew better than pretty much anyone else what needed to be done, but still, that was a lot of balls to keep up in the air.

However, being Victoria, she looked cool and composed in her elbow-sleeved ivory sheath dress, blonde hair pulled back into an impeccable ponytail, clear blue eyes accented by mascara and nothing else. I'd never seen her with a hair out of place, and certainly not when competing in ballroom dance tournaments with Archie, which they still were doing despite their extremely full schedules.

The wedding was set for October fourteenth, a little less than two weeks from now. It wasn't going to be an overly lavish affair, just a small ceremony and reception held in the backyard of the house the couple had purchased about six months ago, but even a modest wedding had a lot of moving parts. Hazel and I would be Victoria's only attendants, since her entire family lived out of state, and she'd been busy enough once her wedding-planning business took off that she'd lost touch with most of her college sorority sisters. I was thrilled to be asked, and I knew Hazel was, too. It meant that Victoria now looked on us as her closest friends, that she was determined to make Globe her adopted hometown as well.

She smiled at me, but I thought I knew her well enough to catch a glimpse of the tension behind that smile. "Oh, I've managed bigger workloads than this," she assured me. "All the same, I'll be glad when Archie and I are safely away in California."

Because, like Calvin and me, the two of them had decided to honeymoon in Sonoma and Napa. I knew choosing that destination had required a bit of wrangling on Archie's part, since at first Victoria had been making noises about possibly going to Cancun.

Problem was, Archie knew he didn't dare leave the country. Calvin, through the means of contacts he didn't want to reveal even to me, had provided Archie with a fake birth certificate and driver's license, along with other bits and pieces of documentation that neatly covered up the reality of his situation.

Namely, that he'd been cursed to live as a cat back in the early 1950s, and therefore didn't have any identification to start a new life as a man in the twenty-first century...well, until Calvin stepped in.

But even though Archie's current documents seemed to serve him just fine in everyday life, he hadn't wanted to put them to the test by trying to get a passport. Maybe Calvin could have gone through the same channels to procure one, but again, doing so might have been tempting fate.

Quite possibly, that was the argument Archie had presented to Victoria to inform her that trying to go out of the country was a bad idea. She knew the truth about who he was, of course, and she'd probably realized they had a good thing going here and shouldn't rock the boat.

"Napa should be beautiful at this time of year," I told her. Calvin and I had gone in early summer, and being in northern California then had also been wonderful, cooler than I'd thought it would be, with fog off the ocean that burned away to mild temperatures, definitely better than the scorching heat of an Arizona June before the monsoon storms began in earnest.

"That's what we're hoping."

Her expression was its usual serene loveliness, not revealing very much of what she might have been thinking. Was she annoyed that they weren't going to Mexico for their honeymoon?

If so, I'd never learn the truth from looking at her.

We exchanged a few more comments about her upcoming trip, and I promised I'd see her on Wednesday at five-thirty as planned. Then she hurried off, saying she needed to head into Mesa to order some blinds. Since I knew her current project required a lot of trips to the greater Phoenix area—little Globe just didn't have the resources to design those homes to her exacting standards—I only smiled and wished her a safe trip.

With any luck, my own day would be equally uneventful.

2

Black Letter

I DIDN'T KNOW WHETHER IT WAS THE WISH I'D sent winging out into the universe or mere luck, but the rest of that Monday was unusually quiet. A busload of tourists came by around two, netting me a couple of hundred bucks in sales, but that was the only significant interruption in my day. Sometimes, if things were slow at the dance studio, Archie would come by and we'd chat for a bit before his next class, and yet I hadn't seen hide nor hair of him today. He'd mentioned something to me just last week that he'd been hired to teach an entire wedding party how to waltz, so maybe that was what occupied him now.

Because I didn't have much else to do with myself, I figured I might as well compose the ad for my shop assistant position. A part of me was oddly reluctant to do so—Once in a Blue Moon was my baby, and I really didn't like the idea of having a stranger working there—but I knew I needed to put my foot-dragging aside and just get on with it. The longer I put it off, the less time I'd have to train the person who'd be taking over for me after I went on leave. Besides, if the first person I hired didn't work out, I'd have more time to find a replacement.

I didn't really like setting myself up for failure from the outset, but I also knew I needed to be practical about the situation.

So I got out the tablet I kept on a shelf under the counter, opened a text document, and started writing.

Full-time sales assistant position now available in historic, scenic Globe, Arizona. Require a responsible, self-starting person to train now and run the shop by themselves in the future. Excellent compensation starting at $25/hour. Position also includes health/dental insurance and paid time off after the first six months.

I paused there, scrunching my nose as I gazed down at the ad and wondered whether I should include that part about vacation time. After all, the whole reason for hiring someone in the first place was to make sure the store stayed open even while I was at home tending to the baby.

Then again, I didn't want to be that person who didn't allow their employees to take time off when necessary. In fact, wasn't some kind of paid leave legally required for someone who worked full-time?

I had to admit I really didn't know what Arizona's laws were on the subject…or the laws of my native California, now that I thought about it. Because I'd been working for myself since I was nineteen and had only had part-time jobs while I was in high school, I honestly didn't have a clue.

Well, better to leave it as-is. Hazel had said she would help out in a pinch, and I supposed Globe wouldn't exactly collapse if its residents had to go a whole week without buying Tarot cards, incense, or a hunk of rock quartz. Besides, the whole point was to make the job sound as enticing as possible, right?

Before I could second-guess myself any further, I navigated to the local Craigslist site, and followed the steps to get the position posted. For just the barest second, my finger hovered over the "submit" button as I wondered if I was really doing the right thing. Maybe I should show Calvin the ad first….

Stop being a baby, I told myself. *Calvin's the one who's been on your case about getting the damn job posted in the first place.*

True enough. I pulled in a breath, then firmly set my finger on the virtual button on the screen.

That was done. Now I'd just have to see what happened next.

A whole lot of nothing, it seemed. All right, I was probably being naïve to think people were so eager to move to Globe that I'd immediately be inundated by applicants, even so, complete radio silence followed the posting of my ad, even though I got a reassuring email from Craigslist letting me know it was now live.

Or maybe that email wasn't quite so reassuring, considering I didn't get a single bite on a job I'd thought sounded pretty good on paper.

Well, there wasn't much point in stewing over it, not when I had months and months to go before I had to step back from my duties at the store. It would have been nice to have the position filled and someone trained sooner rather than later, but it wouldn't be the end of the world if I didn't get someone in here before the first of the year.

Just as four-thirty rolled around and I was puttering around the crystal specimens, carefully cleaning them up with a feather duster I kept for precisely this task, Archie came into the shop.

I opened my mouth to offer him a hello, but then I took a second look at his furrowed brow and realized this probably wasn't merely a casual visit.

He spoke first, thrusting a plain white envelope toward me. "I just got this."

Judging by the expression of consternation he wore, I guessed the contents of the envelope weren't exactly benign. I took it gingerly, noted that it only had the address of Archie's dance studio on the front and no return information, then pulled out the sheet of white paper it held.

A single sentence, in plain black blocky text. Hazel could probably have told me what the font was...not that it really mattered.

I know you're not who you pretend to be.

Cold shivered its way down my spine. "When did you get this?"

"Just now," Archie replied. His jaw was tight, although I could tell he was trying his best to keep his anger and worry in check. As always, he was dressed in khakis and a button-down shirt, although he had the sleeves rolled up as a concession to the warm early autumn day. He had dark blond hair and clear blue eyes, and the chiseled features of a bygone star of the silver screen— appropriate, I supposed, since he'd been born all the way back in the 1920s. "You know the mail always comes here at the end of the day."

True enough. One would have thought that Hank, our local mailman, would deliver the mail downtown first and go on to the residential areas later on, but he didn't work that way. And when I'd once made a comment about his schedule to Josie Woodrow, one of my closest friends in Globe and the town's current mayor, she'd shot me a look of horror and told me that was always how it had been delivered and that I shouldn't rock the boat.

Considering I'd already rocked the boat plenty in Globe, what with my various murder investigations, I figured I'd better let the matter go.

I stared down at those ominous words again. They definitely didn't improve on a second reading.

"Any idea who might have sent you this?" I asked.

Archie's mouth tightened. "Of course not," he snapped. "There's no return address. The letter looks like it was printed on a laser printer, but how many people in the world have one of those?"

Millions, I guessed.

I turned the envelope over. There was no return address, but it had been sent through the U.S. mail, so it at least had a postmark.

"This looks like it was sent from somewhere in Phoenix," I said.

One eyebrow lifted, with Archie appearing singularly unimpressed by that observation. "Yes, I already noticed that," he told me, his tone dripping with annoyance. "Do you have any other valuable insights you'd like to share with me?"

Since I'd known my friend for going on two and a half years by this point, his curt tone didn't rankle the way it might have if I'd been speaking with someone else. "Not really," I said.

His blue eyes narrowed. "You can't sense anything from it?" he asked, now sounding almost desperate. "Any feelings, any flashes?"

"No," I said, but gently. While Archie was a very down-to-earth person—all the Virgo placements in his chart practically guaranteed a no-nonsense outlook on life, despite the way he'd been cursed into a cat body way back when—he'd known me long enough to realize I wasn't exactly your run-of-the-mill person off the street. "I never really had powers like that."

Which was mostly true. Oh, once or twice, I'd picked up on something when I handled an item that was particularly psychically charged, but that dubious talent wasn't anything I could rely on, was even more unpredictable and uncertain than my auras had been.

Rather than become even more irritated at my reply, he let out a breath and seemed to deflate a little. "Then what am I supposed to do about this?"

"Maybe nothing," I said, and once again, his eyebrow cocked.

"Just ignore it?"

"Possibly," I responded. "I mean, it sounds threatening, but it's pretty vague. It's not like they came out and said they know you used to be a cursed cat or anything close to it. This sounds like the kind of crappy blackmail someone would try if they were just fishing."

For a moment, Archie was silent, considering my words. I could only hope I was right in my assessment of the letter, since I was only going on gut feelings and certainly didn't have any actual evidence to back up that reassuring theory.

"If they wanted to blackmail me, why leave it there and not give any details?"

"Because this is probably just the first letter," I said. "Something to get you worried and worked up."

And if that had been the intention of the person who'd sent the letter, then they'd already done a pretty good job.

"So…the next one will be asking for money?" he inquired, jaw tight.

"Maybe," I replied. "I can't say for sure, since I've never been blackmailed. But maybe someone's decided you're a target because you're a new business owner who's been successful."

Archie absorbed my comment for a moment, his golden-brown brows drawn together. "If that's the case, then why hasn't anyone blackmailed you?"

"Well, on the surface, my store doesn't look like much of a moneymaker," I said, which was only the truth. Once in a Blue Moon pulled in just enough to cover the cost of the wares I sold and the electricity and water for the building, but if I hadn't had that inheritance from Lucien Dumond to act as what seemed to be an everlasting backup source of income, I would have been in trouble.

"But everyone knows your money doesn't come from the store," Archie responded, pointing out the obvious.

"Most people in Globe know that," I countered. "It's not the sort of thing I've really advertised, though. And this blackmailer looks like they're from the Phoenix area, so maybe they just thought you were a better target."

Even as I spoke, I realized my words sounded like an overly sunny view of the situation, and I knew I could be dead wrong. After all, Archie's fiancée Victoria was also doing very well for herself, but it didn't appear that anyone had targeted her.

No, the unknown blackmailer had zeroed right in on the one person in town who had some pretty massive secrets to hide.

Judging by the frown that pulled at Archie's

sculpted mouth, I got the feeling he'd been doing the same mental calculations. However, he only said, "Maybe," before adding, "Well, I was hoping you could help, but since it seems as though your gifts aren't going to come to the rescue here, I'd better take this to Victoria and see what she has to say."

"I'm sorry I couldn't do more—" I began, and he waved a hand.

"It's all right," he said. "I suppose I need to remember that I can't expect you to solve all my problems...especially now."

He sent a significant glance at my ever-thickening midsection, then walked out. The bells on the shop door jingled as it closed behind him, sounding far more discordant than they usually did.

I let out a sigh of my own, and wondered if there was something else I could have offered to do for him, something I could have said. Unfortunately, with my talents deserting me...interrupted by my unborn child's "medicine," apparently...I honestly didn't know what else I could have done.

It was only about a quarter to five, but I was finished for the day. I went to the door and locked it, then turned off the lights.

Time to go home.

Calvin was also disturbed to hear about the ominous letter Archie had received. "You say it was postmarked from somewhere in Phoenix?"

"That's what it looked like." I set down my fork, my interest in my plate of pasta carbonara currently dimmed. "Is there a way to fake a postmark?"

"Probably," he replied. Out of deference to my current abstemious state, my husband was also drinking water, and he reached for his glass now as he appeared to ponder the question further. "I mean, people can do all kinds of stuff with Photoshop. But why Phoenix?"

"Maybe to make it look as though the blackmailer is somewhere local?" I suggested. "I know I'd probably be more worried about someone like that lurking nearby than if the postmark was from Kalamazoo, Michigan, or something."

Calvin's mouth twitched a little at my "Kalamazoo" comment. "I suppose that's possible," he said. "But it's probably more likely that this person actually is somewhere in Phoenix. It's a big city, the kind of place where someone could hide easily."

That was for sure. The population of metro Phoenix alone numbered well over a million, and that didn't even count the separate municipalities like Scottsdale and Tempe and Glendale. It would probably be near impossible to track down a single individual there based on one postmark and nothing else.

"Could you dust the envelope for finger-prints?" I asked next.

The smile Calvin sent me was just gently amused enough that I knew it had been a silly question. "That envelope's been handled by way too many people for that to be much use," he said. "The mail carrier, the people at the post office... you and Archie."

Right. Yes, a lot of postal work was auto-mated, but a piece of mail still had to be touched by various people along its route, and that didn't even count the way both Archie and I had care-lessly held the envelope.

"Okay," I said, knowing how dejected I sounded, and picked up my fork again. Even though I had little appetite at the moment, I knew I was eating for two and couldn't afford to let my nervous stomach get the better of me.

Obviously trying to offer some comfort, Calvin commented, "I think you might be right in that someone has gone after Archie because he's a target. Don't forget how visible he is at those ballroom dance competitions."

I hadn't even thought of that. But Archie and Victoria had continued to compete—and win prizes. None of them were as huge as the prizes offered at the Stepping Stars tournament, and yet, five grand here and ten grand there tended to add up. Maybe the person going after my friend was a disgruntled fellow competitor, someone Archie had left in the dust. Considering that he'd only been dancing on the circuit for a little more than a year and had already turned pro and opened his own dance studio, I could see why someone might be jealous enough to call him a fraud and try to extract a little of that prize money from him.

When I explained that theory to Calvin, he nodded. "That sounds about right to me. And for now, there isn't much we can do except wait and see what happens next. Unfortunately, the wording of the letter isn't specific enough to constitute a threat in the eyes of the law. Once they ask for money, then it might be time to approach Henry Lewis."

I couldn't help making a face at the mention of Globe's police chief. True, we'd gone from armed neutrality to guarded friendship—mostly through the efforts of Henry's wife Joyce, whose candles I stocked in my store—but he still took a very dim view of my amateur crime-fighting efforts, despite my so-far perfect track record in figuring out the identities of all those various murderers.

However, he seemed neutral enough about Archie, even though the story we'd told everyone was that Archie was my cousin, who'd moved to

Globe from California. The fictitious relationship hadn't been enough to sour Henry on the subject of Archie Bradshaw, probably because Archie was the polar opposite of my admittedly woo-woo presence in town…and also because Archie hadn't stayed working at Once in a Blue Moon, but had struck out on his own and opened a respectable business just as soon as he could.

"Maybe," I allowed. "Although that will be up to Archie."

And since I knew my friend probably wouldn't want the police poking around for fear they might pull a loose thread on his false identity, unravel it, and realize he wasn't who he was pretending to be, I worried he might try to let the whole thing go, would cave in to the blackmailer's demands.

Well, if that happened, I'd pay the blackmail myself. Over the past couple of years, Archie had become like the brother I'd never had, and I was damned if I was going to let anyone hurt him or try to take away the life and business he'd worked so hard to get.

No, whoever this creep was, they'd learn soon enough that Archie had lots of friends…including one *very* determined hedgewitch.

3

A Helping Hand

"I can't believe this is happening to us," Victoria told me in distressed tones. She'd stopped by the shop at a little past ten the next morning, clearly wanting to get my input on this latest wrinkle in her and Archie's lives.

"It's going to be fine," I assured her, even as I hoped I was telling the truth and that this particular problem was more smoke than fire. "Calvin and I both think it's someone in the ballroom community, someone who's jealous of Archie's success."

Her expression cleared somewhat. Because she was wearing a pretty printed blouse and designer jeans and flats, I guessed she planned to work exclusively in her studio upstairs and didn't have any meetings with clients. Otherwise, she would have been in one of her signature sheath dresses and heels.

"That's what Archie told me at dinner last night," she said. "I want to believe him...but I also don't want to believe a fellow dancer could be so cruel."

Maybe one of my eyebrows lifted a bit. "One of those 'fellow dancers' chopped Brad Masters into pieces and hid him in your steamer trunk."

Victoria shook her head, although I noticed how her mouth tightened at my comment. "All right, but that was an aberration, one person acting alone. It's not like the whole dance community is teeming with murderers and blackmailers."

Probably not. However, even my brief time in the ballroom dance world had shown me there was a lot of backstabbing and catty behavior backstage at those events, so it wasn't too huge a leap of the imagination to think that one of Archie's rivals might have done such a thing to put him off his stride...even if the person who'd printed and mailed that letter didn't have any intention of sliding from innuendo into outright blackmail.

Did they know Archie was getting married in less than two weeks? If so, sending the letter felt that much more cruel. But even leaving that matter aside, the whole thing felt like a very sick joke.

"It would be nice to think that," I told Victoria. "The important thing is to not let this get to you. Whoever mailed that letter is probably hoping for that very thing."

"I know," she replied, and her chin went up a little. Although her gracefully serene presence might have given some people the impression that Victoria was a pushover, I knew nothing could be further from the truth. It took someone with a backbone of steel to handle hundreds of needy brides…and, if I wanted to admit such a thing to myself, to put up with Archie on a daily basis. I loved the man and was happier than I could say that he'd found love after so many years of laboring under that horrible curse, but I knew if I'd been romantically involved with him, I probably would have wanted to push him out a window sooner rather than later. "And I'm just going to keep on with what I've been doing," she added. "Honestly, I've got way too much on my plate right now to let something like this derail me. I'm just glad that I'm working in the office today instead of going out to the site. It's easier to hold it together when I don't have to deal with clients."

Because I'd had my days when I wasn't sure whether I had the intestinal fortitude to handle customers—namely, when Calvin had been accused of murder more than a year and a half ago —I knew exactly how Victoria felt. "Yes, a nice quiet day at the office is exactly what you need," I told her. "Why don't we have lunch together? That should help."

She sent me a grateful smile, even as she shook her head. "I appreciate that," she said. "And normally, I'd say yes. But Archie and I are going out at lunch today to meet with the caterer and finalize a few things."

The last thing I wanted was to get in the middle of any wedding planning details. "Oh, that's fine," I said quickly. "But if you need me to help with anything, just let me know."

"As long as you're at the bridal salon tomorrow at five-thirty, we're good," she assured me. "But now I need to get to work—I have to make some phone calls."

I said that was fine and that I'd see her the next afternoon at the bridal shop as promised, and she hurried out the back entrance of the store so she could climb the stairs to her studio on the second floor.

As soon as she was gone, though, I found myself frowning. I wanted to believe we were correct in supposing this was someone's petty little prank, something designed to put Archie off his stride but definitely not cause any actual damage.

What if it wasn't, though? What if something much worse was going on here?

What if someone really had discovered the truth about Archie's past?

I told myself that was absolutely ridiculous. The reality of his origins was a secret kept by a very small group of people, just Archie and Victoria, Calvin and me. Not even Hazel and Chuck Langdon, two of our closest friends, knew the truth about him. Like everyone else in Globe, they believed he was a cousin from my biological father's side of the family and nothing more. Even my mother accepted that story as the truth, since she'd never asked for child support from my father and hadn't been in contact with him for decades.

Calvin would never, ever betray such a confidence. Neither would Victoria, obviously, and I knew I sure as hell had never uttered a single thing in public about Archie that didn't fit the narrative I'd given everyone else.

So how in the world could anyone have learned there was a little more to Archie Bradshaw than met the eye?

I didn't know. Yes, Calvin had had one of his deputies reach out to make the connections required to get Archie all his false documents, but he'd only told the man that Archie was my cousin and needed a fresh start here in Arizona, hinting that some not very-nice-people in California were looking for him. The deputy seemed to have accepted the story...and besides, everyone who worked at the San Ramon Apache police station was part of the tribe.

If there was one thing the San Ramon coyote shifters were very good at, it was keeping secrets.

Which seemed to send me right back to square one.

It didn't look as though I was going to get any customers anytime soon, so I headed over to the counter that held the cash register and pulled out my tablet. To my surprise, I'd finally gotten a response to my ad on Craigslist, from someone named Melanie Knowles.

Hi, Selena, the email said. *I saw your ad and am very interested in the position. I've attached my resume, along with the contact information for several references. I hope to hear from you soon!*

Well, thank the Goddess. Yes, it was early days yet, but I really wanted to get that shop assistant position filled as fast as possible.

A quick look at her resume told me Melanie had worked in retail for the past eight years, including at some high-end-sounding boutiques in Scottsdale. I wondered why she'd be interested in relocating to Globe, then reminded myself that even fancy stores rarely paid twenty-five bucks an hour to start and include full insurance benefits.

I wanted to write back immediately and ask her when she wanted to come in for an interview, but then I thought maybe it would be a better idea to check her references first. After all, if something sounded off, then I wouldn't have made her drive all the way out to Globe for a face-to-face chat for nothing.

But the first two people I called were both effusive in their praise for the woman, saying she was a hard worker and very conscientious.

"Honestly, I wanted to promote her to assistant manager," the second reference, a woman named Parker Booth, told me. "But she said she needed to cut back on her hours to help her sick grandmother."

Hmm. If Melanie was handling caretaker duties, then would she really be available to move to Globe?

I didn't have the whole story, though, and I figured Melanie could explain the situation to me. Rather than ask any further questions, I thanked Parker for her time, set down the phone, and then got out my tablet again.

Hi, Melanie. Your resume is impressive. Would you be available for an in-person interview either tomorrow or Thursday? I'm flexible on times—whatever works for you.

The answer came back so quickly, it felt as though Melanie Knowles must have been camped on her phone, just waiting to hear from me.

Tomorrow around eleven would be great if that fits in your schedule.

I told her that was perfect, and I'd see her at eleven the next morning.

She thanked me, and that ended our email convo.

As I put the tablet away, I told myself not to get too hopeful. Just because Melanie Knowles looked great on paper didn't mean she would be a good fit for the position. After all, my witchy little shop in out-of-the-way Globe was a far cry from a tony boutique in Scottsdale.

Maybe she was tired of working in a high-end store, though, and ready for a change of pace.

I supposed I'd find out soon enough.

In the back of my mind, I'd been imagining Melanie as someone similar to Victoria, cool and polished in a way I could never be. It was probably silly to be thinking that way, but I supposed it was the Scottsdale connection and the kinds of places Melanie had worked before.

Nothing could have been further from the truth.

Oh, it wasn't that she showed up for the interview in ripped jeans or something, but she was wearing a long black skirt and a simple black elbow-sleeved top, with big silver hoops in her ears and multiple silver rings on her fingers.

In short, she looked exactly like someone who should work in a New Age shop like mine.

She appeared to be around my age, in her early thirties, with hazel eyes and light, sort of fawn-brown hair she wore in the kind of elaborate French braid I knew my own clumsy fingers could never have managed, and was pretty in an understated sort of way.

"Thank you for driving all the way out here," I told her as we shook hands. She sported a French manicure so immaculate that it looked as though she'd had it done in the last day or so.

Wanting to make a good impression?

Probably.

"Oh, the drive wasn't a problem," Melanie told me. "I wanted to come out and look around. I've come through Globe a couple of times, but I've never actually stopped here."

A familiar enough story. My little town wasn't much more than a wide spot in the road or maybe a place to stop for gas for most people, who would be intent on other destinations.

"So, what interests you about relocating to Globe?" I asked, figuring I might as well get to the heart of the matter.

Melanie had been wearing a slight smile during our previous exchange, and it didn't waver now. "I just thought it was time for a chance of pace. I'm kind of tired of big-city life."

Having relocated to Globe from Los Angeles, I could definitely sympathize with that feeling.

"And then I saw your ad," she went on, "and it just felt like the perfect opportunity. I really enjoy working retail, but I didn't think I'd be able to find anything that was such a great fit." She paused there to look around the shop and added, "Your store is really beautiful."

"Thank you," I said, experiencing a little flush of pride. It was a lovely space, thanks to the starry-sky mural my friend Hazel had painted on the ceiling and the displays of crystals and candles and jewelry. In a week or so, I'd haul out the Halloween decorations and work on setting up the "haunted graveyard" scene I'd been putting in the store for the past couple of years, but right now, the only nod to the season was a vase of warm-toned mums that sat on the counter. Since we weren't here to discuss the decor, however, I thought I'd better continue to the real reason why I was looking for an assistant. "I want someone to take over for me next spring when I go on maternity leave, and I figured it was better to get someone in here now so they could be fully trained and able to handle the store on their own."

Maybe Melanie's gaze flickered ever so slightly toward my midsection. I still wasn't showing very much, so that could have been why her expression seemed faintly surprised. Not for the first time, I wished my auras hadn't taken a powder. I could have learned so much from seeing my prospective assistant's aura right then.

But it seemed I wouldn't get that talent back until the baby was born—and maybe not even then—so I knew I had to do what I could with my gut instincts.

And those instincts were telling me Melanie Knowles seemed like a very nice person.

All the same, I knew I'd be remiss if I didn't at least try to act businesslike, even though this was the first time I'd ever interviewed anyone for anything and I had absolutely no idea what I was doing.

Still, I knew enough to ask Melanie about her previous places of employment, and whether she'd ever had to work solo at any of them. She told me that mostly she'd been on a team of at least three people, then added, "But there was one time when two of them were both out sick, so I had to manage the shop on my own for the better part of a week until they were well enough to come back to work."

That sounded good enough to me. After all, I wasn't asking her to handle a busy store with hundreds of customers each day, but a place where I often had only a half dozen or so people come in over the space of the seven hours I was open.

"Any experience with managing inventory or placing orders with vendors?"

"Yes, I did some of that at Jezebel," Melanie replied, naming one of the shops she had listed on her resume.

Well, I didn't think I could ask for much more pertinent experience than that. Every store was a little different, so she'd still have to learn on the job, but otherwise, she seemed absolutely perfect for the position. And if she started now, in early October, she'd have plenty of time to find her bearings before I started my leave at the end of February.

"That all sounds wonderful," I told her, then remembered Parker Booth's comment about Melanie's sick grandmother. "But…is it going to be difficult for your grandmother for you to move so far away?"

The bright, friendly expression Melanie had been wearing immediately disappeared. Her lips pursed, and then she said, "My grandmother passed away a month ago. That's part of the reason why I'm looking for a place to start over."

Oh, dear. I certainly hadn't meant to bring up any painful memories. "I'm so sorry," I murmured.

Her shoulders squared. "It's okay. At least now she isn't suffering anymore."

There really wasn't anything else I could say... well, except the one thing Melanie was probably hoping to hear. "How soon can you start?" I asked.

A faint flush touched her cheeks, and she looked much cheerier than she had only a moment earlier. "So...I'm hired?"

"You are," I said. "I know it might take a while for you to find a place to live, so if you need to wait a week or so—"

"Oh, that's okay," she cut in. "I was actually thinking of renting an Airbnb my first month here while I get acclimated. There's a really cute one over on Oak Street."

My friend Hazel's Airbnb. I wanted to be startled at the coincidence, but told myself it wasn't that big a deal, since Globe didn't have that many vacation rentals to go around. The other ones were all owned by Josie's best friend Mavis.

"Yes, it's very cute," I said. "A friend of mine actually owns that one. I'm sure I could get her to give you a good deal."

"Oh, you don't need to do that—" Melanie began, but I only shook my head.

"No, it's fine. Besides, she always gives a discount to people who rent the place for longer stays, and I know she doesn't have any bookings right now."

"If you're sure…."

"I'm sure," I said firmly. "To be totally honest, I'd love to have you start as soon as possible. Some close friends of mine are getting married a week from Saturday, and knowing someone will be here at the store to cover for me would help a lot in case they need me to run errands for them or whatever."

"I can start tomorrow," Melanie said, then added, "I mean, if we can get the Airbnb thing worked out before then."

"Oh, I know we can," I replied. "Just let me give Hazel a call."

So, while Melanie looked on, I got out my phone and called Hazel, then quickly explained the situation. She was more than happy to accommodate me, since her next booking wasn't until almost Thanksgiving, providing plenty of time for Melanie to stay at the cottage in the interim while she looked for a longer-term rental.

For just a second, I thought it was kind of too bad that I'd already given the upstairs apartment to Victoria for her studio, because it would have been a perfect place for Melanie to land. But no—Victoria was one of my closest friends, and the newly remodeled space had given her a place to work and also meet with clients, one that was centrally located in town and easy to find. Globe wasn't exactly over-brimming with long-term rentals, but I thought I could get Josie on the case, maybe see if there was anyone she knew who'd had a house on the market for a while and might be relieved to have a rental income to cover the mortgage.

There were always solutions to every problem.

"Well, that's settled," I told Melanie after I ended the call with Hazel. "Come back tomorrow, and we can give you the keys to the Airbnb, and then get you started here at the shop."

Melanie was looking a little dazed, something I couldn't exactly blame her for. I kind of doubted she'd expected to walk away from this interview with both her job and her housing so neatly taken care of.

But while I wasn't exactly a take-charge person like Josie, I still preferred to get things handled quickly so I could move on to the next project. And with Melanie on board at the shop, that meant I'd be able to focus on other things, like Archie and Victoria's rapidly approaching nuptials…

…and possibly doing my best to figure out who had sent Archie that threatening note.

"Welcome aboard," I told Melanie, and extended my hand to seal the deal.

4

Fitting Arrangements

"You hired someone already?" Victoria asked, clearly surprised.

She and Hazel and I had all gathered at the bridal salon, where Thora, the owner, had pulled Hazel's and my attendants' dresses. All right, bridesmaid gowns, but since Hazel and I were both in our early thirties and married, and I was carrying my first child, I didn't think there was anything particularly maidenly about either of us. Out of deference to my pregnant state, the gowns had high Empire waists but were absolutely lovely, in a deep blush color with the sort of airy, floaty silk chiffon skirts that made me want to twirl around like a little girl playing dress-up.

Of course, if I tried to twirl right now, I'd probably knock Thora right over, since she was busy with her dressmaker's pins, making a few adjustments to my dress's bodice.

"Yes, and we just had our first day at the shop together," I replied. "I mean, we had to spend most of the morning filling out forms for the insurance and her W-2s and all that. Even so, I thought it went really well."

Which it had. Melanie had come in around nine-thirty, and I'd taken her over to the Airbnb to get settled first, since Hazel had given me the key when I went over the night before after I closed the shop for the day. Once her housing was handled, it was all about filling in those pesky forms my accountant had told me needed to be on file before I could have anyone come work for me. Afterward, though, there was still plenty of time to show Melanie around the shop and point out the various wares, to show her where I kept the key to the display case that held the more expensive jewelry pieces and crystal specimens.

She'd picked up on everything quickly, and revealed more knowledge of gems and minerals than I would have expected of someone who mainly worked in women's wear boutiques.

"Some of them also sold jewelry," she explained. "And I've always kind of liked rocks, so I've done a lot of reading about them on the side."

Not for the first time, I'd reflected it seemed

like the universe had sent me exactly the right person for the job. Although I still had months to go, I knew I was already a little more relaxed than I had been even a few days earlier, now that I knew I had someone like Melanie to take over for me when the time came.

"And she's staying at my Airbnb until she can find a place," Hazel chimed in. She was also wearing her attendant's gown, waiting her turn until Thora was finished with me.

I could kind of tell the bridal salon owner wasn't completely thrilled with the way my body kept changing what felt like from day to day. At least, I was pretty sure I hadn't been quite this booby the last time I'd come in for a fitting.

Luckily, though, Thora was a genius with alterations. All the same, I was very glad the wedding was only a week and a half away. The Goddess only knew what I would have looked like a month from now.

"That's got to be a load off your mind," Victoria said. She looked as calm and put together as always, but I still thought I could detect a certain tension to the set of her shoulders. Because Hazel and I had arrived at the bridal salon at the same time, I really hadn't had the opportunity to speak to Victoria in private, to see if Archie had heard anything else from the blackmailer.

"It is," I said. "Honestly, if everything works out with Melanie the way I think it will, then I might be able to go on leave earlier than I'd planned. I know Calvin would like me to take it easy that final month."

Because although he was never anything except utterly supportive of me, I also could tell he'd be happier—and a lot less worried—if I didn't work until the moment I was practically in labor.

I had to agree with him on that point, and now with Melanie working at the shop, it looked as though I'd have the opportunity to step away whenever it felt right.

"We all would," Hazel remarked. "My mother worked until the day before I was born, and I know she would have done it differently if she could. It's great that you have the luxury of going on leave when it works best for you."

It had been much the same for my own mother, who'd found herself pregnant at barely twenty and didn't have any options except to keep working until she absolutely couldn't.

"Well, now we don't have to worry about me giving birth in front of the incense display at the store," I joked.

Hazel and Victoria exchanged a glance that told me they didn't think my little quip was very funny. In fact, Thora jabbed me with a pin right then, although I didn't know for sure whether that was her way of expressing her disapproval or her finger had just slipped.

Not that I'd ever planned to work that long. Even if I hadn't been able to find a suitable shop assistant, I would have simply closed down the store until I felt ready to go back to work. It wasn't as if I needed the income from Once in a Blue Moon to keep our household going— Calvin's salary as chief of the tribal police was more than sufficient for that, even if you didn't count the interest from all my investments—but I still had never liked the idea of having to keep the store shuttered for months and months.

But it seemed the final pin jab from Thora was a signal she was done with my fitting, because she tapped me on the shoulder and told me I could get down from the dais where I'd been standing so she could move on to Hazel's dress. I obediently stepped away and let Hazel take my place, and went to stand next to Victoria. She'd already done her fitting, and so her wedding gown—a glorious strapless sheath of shantung silk with some fabulous beading on the bodice—had hidden in its garment bag.

"Any developments?" I asked her in an undertone once I was sure Hazel was occupied with Thora.

Victoria shook her head. "No, nothing. I guess that's good news, right?"

"It seems like it to me," I said, once again hoping I was correct about that. "Since you got only the one letter, it sure feels like someone was just trying to get Archie's goat. How's he doing?"

"Fine, I suppose." She stopped there, peach-glossed mouth pursing slightly. "That is, he's just going on with his life, pretending like nothing happened. I'm not sure that's the best way to handle things, but since we haven't heard anything else from whoever sent the letter, it seems like it must have been a mean joke and nothing else."

Part of me wanted to ask what they would do if they received another letter, but I decided that wouldn't be very tactful. No reason to borrow trouble when it looked—for now, at least—that the letter-writer had decided it was enough to give Archie that one poke and then run away.

"And he's still not going to have a bachelor party?" I asked next, figuring it was probably better to change the subject, especially since Hazel had shifted on the dais and could now see and hear us a little more clearly.

That question earned me two lifted brows. "What do you think?"

I thought Archie would probably prefer getting sent back into a cat's body than have to suffer the indignity of being seen at a "gentleman's club." "Okay, stupid question," I replied with a grin. "I just wanted to check because Calvin asked me last night. He said he and Chuck would be fine with just going out for a drink or something, nothing too crazy. I mean, we girls are all having a spa day together next week. It seems like the guys should do something to celebrate, too."

For a moment, Victoria didn't reply, and I worried maybe she was going to shoot down something as innocent as having a drink or two at the bar in the Gold Dust, the casino the San Ramon tribe operated just past the eastern edge of Globe. But then she gave a very small lift of her shoulders and said, "I'll ask him. He might be willing to do something like that."

I didn't exactly let out a sigh of relief, but I was glad to hear Archie might be open to the idea of doing at least a little something to celebrate his last few days as a single man. For him, the idea of being married must carry a special significance. Not just because he'd spent so many years as a cat, but because for most of his adult life, he hadn't experienced physical attraction to anyone and had thought he must be asexual.

It turned out that he was actually demisexual, a person who was attracted to one special individual and no one else, and it had taken all those decades in a cat body to bring him to the time when he'd finally met Victoria and fallen immediately in love. For a man who'd spent most of his life thinking he would always be alone, realizing that he was going to be married in less than ten days had to hold some massive significance.

"Good," I said. "Just have him call Calvin when he decides, and then Calvin can set something up."

By "setting something up," I meant Calvin could probably get the casino's private VIP room for the evening, so the guys could have their drinks in comfort without having to worry about having their little party intruded on by drunken tourists, or whatever. It wasn't as if I thought my husband would hire a few strippers for the night, something that would probably make Chuck laugh but would embarrass Archie for all eternity.

"I will," Victoria promised.

Hazel's gown required a lot fewer alterations than mine had, so Thora finished up with her right then, telling both of us we could get back into our street clothes, but to be careful about the pins in our bodices. We retreated into separate dressing rooms, extricated ourselves, and got back into the outfits we'd been wearing when we arrived at the bridal salon.

"Want to go grab a snack?" Hazel suggested once we'd all reconvened by the salon's front door.

"Wish I could," Victoria said. "But my client sent over some change orders right as I was leaving to meet you here, so I need to go back to the studio and make some notes."

The expression Hazel wore then was more resigned than anything else, as if she'd already been expecting that kind of response. She and Victoria got along well enough, but Victoria was way more Type A and driven than Hazel, and I knew sometimes she had a hard time relating to the way Victoria always put work first.

"But I'm down for some tacos," I said quickly. "Calvin's working until nine today, so I would have been on my own for dinner, anyway."

"You two have fun," Victoria told us. "Eat a taco for me."

"Better not," I replied with a grin. "I can't gain too much weight between now and next Saturday, or Thora will kill me."

Victoria chuckled, as I'd hoped she would, then promised again that she'd have Archie reach out to Calvin once he'd decided what he wanted to do about his guys' night out.

Because our favorite Mexican restaurant, Olamendi's, was walking distance from the salon, Hazel and I headed over there on foot.

"Just one taco for me," she said after we were seated at a table. "I've got some stew in the crock pot at home."

"Look at you, being all domestic and stuff," I replied with a smile.

She only shook her head. "Well, it didn't seem fair to have Chuck cook all the time, so I've taught myself a few things. I'm never going to be Ms. Cordon Bleu like you are."

I didn't bother to protest that description, because I really loved to cook and enjoyed coming up with new dishes to tempt Calvin's palate. Now all I had to do was hope our baby wouldn't grow up to be one of those kids who subsisted solely on chicken nuggets and macaroni and cheese, and nothing else.

"Well, thanks for keeping me company while I chow down on tacos," I said. "I could've heated something up, I suppose, but this is a lot more fun."

Hazel shrugged. "Hey, it was my suggestion. And Chuck and I won't be eating until after seven, so I'll have time to process my one taco."

And chips, I thought, as Rosa, one of the restaurant's owners, set a basket of tortilla chips and a little bowl of salsa down on the table. She took our orders, said she'd be out with some water shortly, and then headed back into the kitchen.

"So, you had a good first day with Melanie?" Hazel asked.

"Yes, it all went great," I replied. "Thanks again for letting her stay at your Airbnb until she can find something more permanent."

Hazel reached for a chip, dunked it in some

salsa, and took a bite. "Hey, you're doing me a favor," she said after she was done chewing. "Otherwise, the place would've been sitting empty for almost a month."

True enough, but still, she'd come through for Melanie—and me—and that meant a lot. I ventured, "Would you consider turning the house into a long-term rental if Melanie has a hard time finding a place to go?"

Hazel tilted her head to one side, considering my question. "Maybe," she said after a long pause. "I wasn't sure I wanted to take that plunge, but the truth is, I'm not renting the place as often as I'd hoped I would. Mavis has been renting her houses a lot longer than I have, so she has more reviews and is a Superhost, and it seems like people gravitate toward her properties because of that."

I hadn't even considered that aspect of the situation, but, to be fair, I didn't know a lot about the ins and outs of running an Airbnb. "I'm sorry," I said. "I didn't know you were having such a hard time with it."

Hazel shrugged, but waited to say anything until Rosa had set our glasses of water on the table, taken our taco order, and then departed once again. "If I were really relying on that income," she replied, "I'd be more worried about it. But Chuck owns the ranch free and clear because of his parents leaving it to him, and my art is really taking off, so renting out the cottage is more of a side thing than anything else."

"Well, just let me know," I said, glad to hear that her Airbnb's lack of success wasn't a make-or-break element of her finances.

Hazel gave me a brief nod, then pursed her mouth slightly. "It seems like you're going out of your way to make sure everything works out with Melanie."

Maybe I was. But it was such a relief to have her there at the shop, to know that if things continued to go well, I'd have the freedom to go on maternity leave earlier than I'd planned, to schedule doctor's visits without having to worry about trying to set them up either before or after I got off work. Now, if I absolutely had to drive into Mesa for a special test or something in the middle of the day, it wouldn't make a huge difference one way or another.

"Well, I remember what it was like to look for housing back in L.A.," I replied. "And it was a total pain."

A quick flash of a smile. "I can believe that. But don't worry—I definitely won't be charging L.A. prices for my house."

No, probably not. Even the Phoenix rental market was pretty crazy these days…at least, that's what I'd heard…but no one could get away with demanding those kinds of rents in a quiet little backwater like Globe. There were a few people in town who commuted into Phoenix's eastern suburbs, like Gilbert or Mesa, although they were definitely the minority. We just weren't close enough to be considered a bedroom community for the sprawling megalopolis, and that meant the housing prices here were still pretty reasonable.

Rosa came by with our tacos then, and Hazel and I went on to chat about Archie and Victoria's upcoming wedding, and a new gallery show Hazel would be putting on in late October, in a gallery in Gilbert whose owner had really taken a shine to her paintings. All ordinary enough topics, and yet I couldn't quite ignore the stream of unease that ran beneath the surface of our conversation. For now, it seemed as if the blackmailer had held off, but what if he was holding back, just waiting to strike at a time that would cause the most trouble for my friends and their rapidly approaching nuptials? After all, you couldn't rely on someone like that to show any compassion, or they would never have written that letter in the first place.

Luckily, Hazel didn't seem to notice anything off about my expression or my tone of voice, and after we finished our snack, she gave me a quick smile and told me she'd see me next Wednesday for our girls' spa day, if not sooner.

As I waved goodbye, another of those unsettling shivers of cold ran down my back, and I forced myself to smile in return. Maybe my auras were still on vacation in the Bahamas, but my sixth sense seemed to be telling me we might not be meeting for that spa day after all....

5

Scream in My Coffee

I said nothing to Calvin about my misgivings, however. For one thing, I had absolutely nothing to go on, just an overall sensation of foreboding, and for another, I knew I was pumped full of pregnancy hormones and could simply be imagining things. After all, if I'd lost my ability to see auras, maybe my gut feelings were nothing more than my body experiencing yet another change as I moved through my fourth month of pregnancy.

That Thursday at the store was quiet, so I took advantage of the downtime to walk Melanie through my inventory system and coach her as she placed an order with one of my vendors to get some more incense, which had gotten depleted lately by the local high school girls, who descended on the fragrant cones and sticks with frightening regularity. My new assistant seemed to pick up on everything with ease, telling me that not only did she already have experience with this sort of thing, but was smart enough to overcome the differences between the way I handled inventory and how it had been done at the previous places where she'd worked.

"And how's the house working out for you?" I asked after she'd run down the street to Cloud Coffee to get us some sandwiches and iced green teas. My doctor had told me it was all right for me to have the mildly caffeinated drink every once in a while, and since I'd had a restless night the evening before, I was definitely in need of a little pick-me-up.

"Oh, great," Melanie replied at once as she handed over my tea, followed by a ham and swiss croissant. "The house is really cute. Tell your friend Hazel thanks again for letting me stay there."

That was just about what I'd expected to hear, because Hazel's cottage was absolutely adorable in every way. Still, I was glad to hear Melanie approved of it as well. "How would you feel about staying there permanently?"

As soon as I asked the question, Melanie's eyes widened. "Seriously? I thought it was just an Airbnb."

"It is," I replied. "But Hazel's been thinking for a while that it might be better for her to switch it over to a long-term rental."

"That would be fabulous," Melanie breathed, then sipped some of her iced latte. However, her expression slipped a little as she added, "But wouldn't a furnished place like that be pretty expensive?"

"I don't think so," I assured her. "Rents here in Globe are probably a lot more reasonable than what you're used to. But Hazel's still thinking about it, so I don't think she's even settled on a price yet."

"I can give her whatever references she needs," Melanie said quickly. "Luckily, the last place I lived was just month-to-month, so it was easy to get out of the rental agreement and come here."

Yes, that was pretty handy. As I knew all too well from my time living in Los Angeles, it could get really tricky trying to find a new place that would line up with the day when your current lease ended. She was lucky that she'd been living in an apartment that had allowed the flexibility of a month-to-month agreement.

"Right now, we're both pretty busy because of our friend's wedding on the fourteenth," I said. "But after that, I'll see if Hazel has figured out what she wants to do about the cottage."

Melanie seemed agreeable to that plan, and we

ate our sandwiches quickly, just in case we might get some post-lunch shoppers. I supposed I should have set up some kind of lunch schedule so she wouldn't be on the clock the whole time, but I had to admit I hadn't even thought about that. When I was working on my own, I took a lunch break whenever it felt right, and hung up my little "be back at" sign so I could go grab something from Cloud Coffee or whatever, but legally, my assistant needed at least a half-hour official lunch, and fifteen-minute breaks in the morning and afternoon.

"Sorry about this," I said as she dropped her sandwich wrapper in the trash, and she gave me a questioning look.

"About what?"

"About not figuring out your lunch schedule. Is a half hour all right? I thought maybe you could take your lunch from twelve to twelve-thirty, and then I could take mine from twelve-thirty to one."

For a second, Melanie looked blank, and then she gave me a reassuring smile. "Oh, right. I hadn't even thought about that. Working here feels so relaxing, it hardly seems like a job to me."

Her comment made a happy little rush go through me. I supposed some people liked to micro-manage and got an unhealthy kick out of being the boss from hell, but not me. That

Melanie felt so relaxed at Once in a Blue Moon told me I'd created exactly the working environment for her I'd hoped for.

We had a few customers come in that afternoon, just enough to keep us both busy. All the same, I told Melanie she could leave an hour early if she needed to, since she'd made a comment earlier that day about how she still needed to head back to Phoenix and retrieve a few odds and ends from her apartment, since she'd prorated the rent there to keep the place through today, allowing her enough time to get it cleared out.

She thanked me and hurried out back, where I knew her older-model Toyota Camry was parked near my Jeep Renegade. No sooner than I'd begun to putter around the book display, re-shelving a couple of volumes that had been put back in the wrong place, Victoria came through the back entrance to the shop, her expression distressed.

In her hand was a white envelope, and my heart sank.

"You got another one?" I asked as she approached, and she nodded.

"Was it that obvious?"

"Between the look on your face and that"—I nodded at the envelope she held—"I didn't know what else it could be."

She pulled in a breath. Because she was

wearing one of her signature sheath dresses, this one in a mid-toned blue that went perfectly with her eyes, I guessed she must have had a meeting with the developers of the project whose model homes she was designing.

I could only hope she'd received the letter after that meeting.

"Yes, it just came in the mail…my studio mail," she clarified, just in case there was any doubt as to where the letter had been sent. Then she opened the envelope and pulled out the single sheet of white paper it contained. "*I know about your fiancé,*" she read. "*I'll meet with you in your studio at ten the morning of October sixth to list my demands. Say nothing to Mr. Bradshaw…or the police.*"

An oddly formal blackmailer. However, I brushed that data point aside and said, "He wants to meet you in person? That seems strange."

"I know," Victoria replied. "Isn't the whole point of blackmail remaining anonymous?"

"You'd think so," I said. "Not that I have a lot of experience in that department."

She made a distracted little waving movement with the hand that held the letter, as if to show she had no idea what to make of it, either. "What should I do?"

I had a ready answer to that question. "You need to call Henry Lewis."

At once, her mouth turned down. "The letter says I'm not supposed to involve the police. What if the blackmailer has an accomplice who's going to do something terrible to Archie if I don't go along with his demands?"

Yikes. I hadn't even thought about that possible scenario, but it made some sense. Or at least, it seemed more likely the blackmailer felt comfortable making these demands because he had an ace in the hole in the form of an accomplice who was happy to carry out his dirty work.

"Still…." I said, then paused as an idea began to form in my mind. "What if I ask Calvin to be here tomorrow morning? He's not local police, so there's only so much he can do in a place that's not his jurisdiction, but I'd feel a lot better about you meeting with this creep if Calvin was here at the shop. That way, he could be there to get a look at him, maybe follow him to see where he goes afterward. Then we can decide whether we need to go to the regular Globe P.D. or not."

Victoria's expression had slowly brightened as she listened to my suggestion…but then dimmed again. "Are you sure Calvin will be okay with that?"

"Absolutely," I replied without hesitation, even as I uttered a silent prayer that he actually would be on board with my plan. "He doesn't have to be at work until noon tomorrow, so his morning is free. He can drive over with me, and that way, there won't be a tribal police vehicle parked anywhere nearby. It'll be fine."

A few seconds passed as Victoria appeared to absorb that information. "Okay," she said after a pause. "I think that'll work. And I have to admit, I'll feel a lot better about meeting this person if I know Calvin is down here with you."

"And if anything goes sideways," I told her, "just have a text ready to go, and Calvin can be upstairs in less than a minute."

Her chin went up, and she nodded. "Sounds like a plan." Another hesitation, and then she went on, "And thank you for not trying to convince me I should tell Archie about all this."

"If I didn't have Calvin ready to come to the rescue, I might feel differently about the situation," I said frankly. "But as it is, it just seems better to keep Archie out of it until the meeting is over. Knowing him, he'd try to interfere, and the letter seems pretty clear about not wanting him anywhere near your studio tomorrow morning."

Victoria sent me a grateful smile. "Thank you for helping out," she told me. "Knowing that Calvin is going to be here makes me feel a lot better about all this."

"No problem," I assured her…even as I hoped it really wouldn't be.

Calvin stared at me from across the dinner table, clearly perturbed by the story I'd just related. "You know you should have had Victoria call Henry," he said, in tones that told me he wasn't nearly as thrilled with Victoria's and my plan as I'd hoped he would be.

"And have him come bumbling in and make a total hash of things?" I countered as I broke off a piece of biscuit. "No way."

My husband didn't seem very convinced by this argument. "Henry Lewis is not as much of a bumbler as you think he is," he said, level black brows drawing together. "Yes, he might have dropped the ball a couple of times over the years, but he's still a competent cop."

I made a noncommittal noise as I buttered my biscuit. That night I'd had a craving for fried chicken, so that's what we were eating, along with homemade macaroni and cheese...and a green salad, just so the entire meal wouldn't be a completely indulgent calorie-fest. "So competent that I've solved nine murders since I moved to Globe and he didn't help with a single one?"

"He helped arrest Thad Sullivan," Calvin pointed out.

Okay, that was true. Henry—and two of his deputies—had apprehended Mr. Sullivan, but only because he was working off a tip I'd given him. Otherwise, I doubted he would have ever figured out that reality star Dillon James had been offed by his own producer.

"So I'll give him a point for that," I said. "That doesn't mean either Victoria or I want him there tomorrow, especially since that letter she got specifically stated there shouldn't be any police involvement. Since you're not a member of the Globe P.D., it puts you in kind of a gray area, right?"

Calvin's mouth tightened a bit. "Maybe, if you want to split hairs. I'm not sure your blackmailer will see it that way."

"And he doesn't have to," I said serenely. "You'll be in my shop in civilian clothes, so even if he catches a glimpse of you before he heads up to Victoria's studio, he's not going to think you're anything except another customer. Ditto for when we'll tail him after he leaves."

"'We'?" my husband repeated, now looking a little alarmed.

"Well, obviously," I replied before taking a bite of biscuit. I swallowed the morsel, then added, "I have to drive you back home to get your Durango anyway, so I figured we'd go together and see where the guy is headed."

"Leaving your new employee to watch the

store without you when she's barely been there for three days," he observed, his tone now dry.

"Melanie can handle it," I said. There might have been a lot of holes in my plan, but I knew that part of it was solid. My assistant had already shown that she had a firm grasp of the regular day-to-day duties required for working at Once in a Blue Moon, so I knew for a fact she'd be able to fly solo for an hour or two, especially since this was a quiet time of year for me.

A long pause as Calvin appeared to weigh my reply and decide whether he wanted to protest further, or whether he should go ahead and cave since it was obvious that I had an argument to counter any protests he might make on the subject.

It looked like he'd decided on the latter course, because he only said, "All right. I still don't like it, but…."

He let the syllable hang in the air, and I nodded.

"It's all going to be fine," I assured him.

"I'm not so sure about that," he replied, then leaned over in his chair so he could feed our Chihuahua mix Sadie a bit of chicken with the skin pulled off. "But I guess we'll just have to wait and see."

And that seemed to be that.

I had to admit I couldn't ignore the nervous little quivers in my stomach as Calvin and I entered the shop the next morning, even though I would have preferred to believe their source was the baby moving, rather than my own qualms over the plan Victoria and I had put together. Her red Mercedes SUV was already parked out back, telling me she'd probably gotten here early to give herself extra time to prepare for the upcoming meeting…and maybe make herself a second cup of tea to shore up her spirits.

Melanie wasn't here yet, but since we'd pulled into the parking lot at about a quarter 'til, I wasn't too surprised by that. I hadn't gotten around to having a second set of keys made for her, so it only made sense that she'd wait until closer to opening so she'd know I was already at the store to let her in.

Sure enough, she arrived at about five minutes until ten, and sent a slightly startled glance toward Calvin, who was looking at the various volumes on the bookshelves and trying to appear inconspicuous. That sort of thing was nearly impossible for him, mostly because he stood six foot five in his sock feet and had long black hair that hung to his waist, but I could tell he was still making the attempt, anyway.

Before the moment could get too awkward, I said, "Melanie, this is my husband, Calvin. He came with me to work because his car is in the shop, and I needed to come over and get things unlocked here before I could drive him to the mechanic to pick it up."

There, that story sounded plausible enough. I'd concocted it on the way over here, thinking I needed to provide some sort of excuse to explain why my husband was loitering around the store.

He stepped away from the bookcase and extended a hand. "Very nice to meet you, Melanie," he said.

"Nice to meet you, too," she replied, looking a little dazed. She knew I was married, but she probably hadn't guessed that my husband was nearly six and a half feet of utter indigenous gorgeousness.

"His car's supposed to be ready around ten-thirty," I went on. "We're just waiting for a text from the mechanic. Then I'll have to step out for a bit to drive him over there, but I shouldn't be gone too long."

"Oh, that's fine," Melanie said stoutly. "I can cover for you here for as long as you need."

During that exchange, Calvin's gaze had flickered almost imperceptibly toward the rear entrance of the store. When I'd first bought the building, there had only been a door that opened onto the parking lot and a storage area immediately inside, but after I'd given Victoria the apartment upstairs, she'd remodeled that space into an actual foyer, with a glass door that allowed access to Once in a Blue Moon and a set of stairs that led up to her second-floor studio. After the remodel was completed, we'd discussed getting security cameras, but then had decided that probably wasn't necessary in sleepy little Globe, and had settled for only an alarm system instead.

I guessed that the quick shift of my husband's eyes toward the little lobby area was a signal that our blackmailer had arrived and was going up the stairs toward Parrish Design.

Another nervous thrill went through me, but I did my best not to react, not to show that I'd guessed anything out of the ordinary was taking place in the studio upstairs.

"Thanks for that, Melanie," I said, glad I sounded casual and composed. "I didn't mean to have you handling things on your own here so soon after you got started, but, like I said, I shouldn't be gone for very long."

"Think I'm going to get a bottle of water from the fridge," Calvin said, also completely at ease. The little break room tucked into my storage area had a mini fridge, a place where I kept some bottled water and any leftovers I might have brought to work for those times when I didn't feel like getting takeout for lunch.

"Sure," I replied with a smile. Maybe he really was thirsty...but I thought it far more likely that he wanted an excuse to position himself as close to the rear entrance as possible so he'd be able to head out quickly once the blackmailer came back down the stairs.

I wasn't sure what excuse I'd need to concoct to explain why I would go running after him in that event, but I supposed I'd figure it out on the fly.

As it was, I had to do my best to act natural as I went over to the front door and unlocked it, then took down the "be back at" sign in the front window. That task done, I headed over to the counter where the cash register was located, and mentioned casually to Melanie that she might as well dust the crystals while the shop was still quiet.

She nodded, retrieved the feather duster, and went to the crystal display. During all of this, I was intensely aware of the minutes ticking past, my mind racing as it conjured scenarios of what might be happening in Victoria's studio right overhead. Was the blackmailer threatening her? Was she pleading with him to understand that her wedding was now only a week away, and there was nothing about Archie that warranted this kind of terrible threat?

I didn't know. All I knew was that when my phone rang from inside my skirt pocket—I'd stashed it there so I wouldn't have to go running back toward the place where my purse was hidden under the counter—I felt like I jumped about a foot.

That iPhone was in my hand so fast, I might have conjured it with a snap of my fingers.

Victoria's number.

"S-Selena?" she said, her voice shaking.

"What's the matter?" I replied at once, fear thrilling along every nerve ending as I imagined the worst. "What happened?"

A pause. Then she said, still in those tremulous tones, "I-I think you and Calvin had better come up here."

Victoria never sounded like that. Sometimes I thought it would take a bomb going off in the immediate vicinity for her to lose her cool. That was why I didn't ask any questions, only said, "We'll be there in a sec."

"Thank you."

I ended the call, stuck my phone back in my pocket, and looked over at Melanie, who was carefully swishing away any dust that might have collected on the minerals clustered on their display table. "I need to go upstairs for a minute," I said. "Just be a sec."

"No problem," she responded sunnily, clearly unaware of whatever drama might have gone down in the studio upstairs.

I hurried toward the back of the store. Calvin, who was drinking from the bottle of water he'd fetched a moment earlier, lowered the bottle from his mouth and looked at me in surprise.

"Victoria needs us upstairs," I said briefly.

No questions, because Calvin was just like that. Instead, he followed me out of the shop as I hurried up the flight of steps that led to a small landing just outside Victoria's design studio. The door was shut but not locked—usual for business hours—so I opened and it went inside, my husband still on my heels.

Immediately inside the door was a small waiting area, what used to be the dining room when I'd lived in the apartment. Victoria had downsized the kitchen but kept a small refrigerator, sink, and cabinets, presumably so she could offer her clients refreshments when they came in for an appointment.

The former living room had been set up as a conference area, with a round table in the center of the space and open shelving on the wall facing the fireplace. Victoria stood in front of that table, her face utterly white. On the polished wood floor just off to one side lay the prone body of a man, a blue-glazed coffee cup still clutched in one hand, with pale mocha liquid spreading out beneath both the cup and his head.

"I don't know what happened," she said simply.

6

Non-Dairy Screamer

HENRY LEWIS WORE THE EXPRESSION OF A man who would have liked nothing more than to kick Calvin and me right out of the room. However, since Victoria had insisted on us being present during this interview, he couldn't do much more than shoot the two of us a narrow gaze out of his flinty gray eyes, eyes that almost matched his short-cropped hair.

They had already carried away the victim on a stretcher, thank the Goddess. I'd only caught a quick glimpse of a sharp-featured man who looked as though he was probably in his early or mid-thirties, with dark hair and a thin dark mustache above his mouth, before the EMTs took him out of Victoria's studio...presumably to the medical examiner's so they could figure out just what the heck had made him drop dead on the spot like that.

The four of us were standing in what used to be my master bedroom when Victoria's studio was still my apartment, although it was now clearly the place where she did most of her creating. A drafting table with a sketchbook open to a half-finished living room design occupied the wall where my bed had once been placed, and the wall opposite it was covered with mood boards and tacked-up swatches of fabric. Since there was only one chair, the one placed in front of the table, we'd been forced to awkwardly occupy the center of the space.

"You said the man was blackmailing you?" Henry inquired. "Why?"

"I—I don't know," Victoria replied. She pressed her lips together and pulled in a breath. "He said he knew something about me and Archie, which is just ridiculous. We have nothing to hide."

I had to reflect that she was an excellent actress, because her current air of utter mystification would have fooled me if I hadn't known exactly what Archie was hiding. Chief Lewis only nodded, which didn't tell me very much.

Had he bought her innocent act?

"Meeting with someone like that is dangerous," he said next, echoing Calvin's own view of the situation.

"I know," Victoria said. "But I had Calvin downstairs, so I figured I would be safe enough."

A brief pause as the police chief sent my husband a disapproving glance, as if to tell him he'd really dropped the ball by agreeing to be part of such a dodgy scheme. Calvin, luckily, was one of those people who could remain utterly impassive no matter what might be going on around him, so he didn't even respond, only continued to gaze back at Henry without so much as a blink.

"All right," Henry said dryly. "So you thought you had backup. Why don't you tell me exactly what happened?"

She swallowed. "I think I need some water."

"I'll get it," I offered, and headed for the door, which we'd left open to the hallway, then went out into the studio's primary space. Although the layout of the kitchen had changed a little, I still quickly located a glass and poured Victoria some water from the pitcher in the fridge. Once I was done with that task, I went back to the room where everyone was waiting for me. I handed her the water, and she took a sip.

"The blackmailer sent me a letter saying he was going to meet me here at ten o'clock today," she said.

"Do you have this letter?" Henry asked.

She nodded. "It's in my office across the hall. Do you want me to get it?"

"Not right now," he replied immediately. "You can hand it over as evidence once we're done with this interview. So, the blackmailer demanded a meeting. Was this the first time you'd heard from him?"

"No," she said. "He sent a letter to Archie's studio a couple of days earlier, but it wasn't as specific."

"What did it say?"

For a moment, she hesitated, her gaze moving to Calvin for just the barest second. He gave her a very small nod, as if to let her know she might as well tell Henry what the first letter had contained, since he was going to find out soon enough, anyway.

"It said, 'I know you're not who you pretend to be.'"

One of Henry's eyebrows lifted ever so slightly. "Any idea what that was supposed to mean?"

Victoria crossed her arms. The vintage diamond Archie had given her twinkled from her left hand, reminding me—and probably Calvin as well—that this had to be some of the worst timing ever.

"No," she said. Her gaze was forthright, and again, I would have completely bought her story if I hadn't known exactly what she and Archie were keeping secret from the rest of the world. "But we think it might have something to do with his dance studio, with all the dance tournaments we've competed in. Usually, it takes years and years before people turn pro and become instructors, but Archie did it in less than a year and a half."

"I had no idea he was such a prodigy," Henry remarked, lip curling ever so slightly.

If the situation hadn't been so serious, I would have shot him a disapproving look at that disparaging remark. As it was, I could only stand there and hope I was being as stony-faced as my husband.

"He's a remarkable dancer," Victoria said, with an admirable evenness to her tone. "He had dance lessons from an early age, so his turning pro in that time span only seems unbelievable to people who don't know his history. Anyway, we thought the first letter was someone just trying to mess with him, to put him off balance so he might make a mistake in our next competition."

Henry shifted his weight from one foot to the other, his expression still nothing more than mildly curious. "But then you got the second letter from the blackmailer, the one asking to meet with you."

"Yes."

"Did you tell Mr. Bradshaw about it?"

"No," she responded, and once again, the police chief lifted an eyebrow.

"Why not?"

"Because I didn't want to upset him, not with our wedding so close," Victoria said. "I thought that with Calvin and Selena here as backup, I'd be able to handle whatever happened."

"Apparently not," Henry commented, still in a tone as dry as the dusty hills outside town.

Victoria drew in a breath and looked as if she wanted to make some kind of tart reply. But then she seemed to realize that snapping at Henry Lewis wasn't a very good idea, so she just released the breath she'd pulled in a second earlier and said, "No, I guess not."

"Tell me exactly what happened."

She hesitated for a moment, then said, "The man got here a little after ten."

"'The man'?" Henry cut in. "He didn't tell you his name?"

"No," she said. "He probably didn't see the need to give me any more information than was strictly necessary."

"You'd think if he wanted to hide his identity, he wouldn't have met with you in person."

"You would think," Victoria responded, tone now a little tart. "I don't know what his reasoning was. And unfortunately, we can't ask him, because he's dead."

Henry's lips thinned. "That's true," he said. "So, the man—we'll call him John Doe for now—came to your studio. What happened next?"

"I was trying to be polite," she said. "I asked him he wanted coffee or tea, or water. He told me he wanted coffee and asked if I had any creamer. I told him I did, then went into the kitchen and made him a cup with my Keurig. After that, I got the container of creamer from the fridge and poured some into his coffee. I took him the coffee, and he drank a couple of swallows, then fell to the floor, dead. That's when I called Selena and Calvin."

The police chief looked even less thrilled by this reminder of our involvement in the whole mess. As for me, I couldn't quite ignore the cold sensation in the pit of my stomach. A little less than a year ago, the televangelist Aaron Galloway had also dropped dead after drinking a cup of coffee provided by a friend of mine. In that case, suspicion had centered on Josie...until it was proven that Mark Lemmon, a local man furious that his wife had squandered their life savings by sending massive donations to the TV preacher, had murdered that Pastor Galloway.

But when Aaron Galloway had died, the poison was arsenic, something that had given him violent stomach cramps until he passed away a few hours later. He definitely hadn't dropped dead on the spot the way Victoria's nameless black-mailer had.

The man had obviously been poisoned, but with what? What kind of toxin acted that fast? Cyanide? Strychnine?

Since I hadn't exactly made a study of the subject, I had no idea.

"I'll need to see that creamer," Henry Lewis said, his tone grim.

"It's in the fridge," Victoria told him. "I can go get it—"

"No," he cut in immediately. "I don't want you handling it any more than you already have."

He left the design space and went into the kitchen, pulling a pair of rubber gloves out of his pocket as he went. Standing a few feet away from Calvin and me, Victoria sent us a single stricken glance, one that told us she'd already done the mental math and was coming up with a sum she didn't like very much.

I had to admit that if I hadn't known she was utterly blameless in all this, I would have thought she must be the one who'd killed the blackmailer. After all, what better motive for murder than the pressing need to get rid of someone threatening to ruin your life less than a week before your wedding?

Whatever was in that creamer, though, I knew Victoria hadn't put it there any more than I had.

As though we were all acting according to some unspoken agreement, the three of us trailed along behind Henry and back out into the studio's main room, which was now empty. It looked as though his deputies had finished gathering whatever evidence they could find; a place as small as Globe didn't exactly have what you could call a dedicated forensics team.

The police chief went to the refrigerator, pulled a pair of latex gloves out of his pocket, and slid them on before opening the door. He took out the innocent-looking carton of creamer, set it on the counter, then got out his phone.

"Deputy," he said, "I've got some evidence here that needs to be collected. Come up to Ms. Parrish's studio and get it, then take it to the station to be admitted."

Did the Globe P.D.'s evidence locker have a refrigerated section?

I didn't dare ask, obviously. No, I just had to stand there and wait with Victoria and Calvin until the deputy—one of the men who'd been there when Henry arrested Thad Sullivan, Dillon James' murderer, although I still didn't know his name—appeared at the studio door. Still wearing the rubber gloves, Henry placed the container of creamer in the baggie the deputy had produced and told the man to hurry.

The deputy nodded and, baggie of evidence in

hand, hurried back down the steps, no doubt to get the creamer to the station as quickly as possible.

Was Henry worried that the poison might break down if the liquid inside the little wax-coated paper carton came up to room temperature?

Again, I didn't know. I wasn't sure whether Calvin would know, either, even though he'd taken a class on poisons and other toxins when getting his degree in criminal justice at Arizona State University.

I'd have to ask him once we were alone.

Henry turned back toward Victoria, still wearing that grim expression. Before he could say anything, Archie burst into the room, looking more frantic than I'd ever seen him.

"What happened?" he exclaimed as his gaze moved right to Victoria where she stood a few feet away from the kitchen. "Victoria, are you all right?"

"I'm fine," she said, although her tone was understandably tight. "I'll explain later."

"*Much* later," Henry said, eyes as flinty as ever. "Victoria Parrish, I'm afraid I'm going to have to arrest you for the murder of John Doe."

I supposed there was one good thing about getting arrested early in the morning on a weekday. At least this time, the judge could hear the preliminary evidence and decide Victoria only needed a hundred grand to get bailed out, probably because she had no priors and the evidence against her was kind of flimsy. Maybe that would change once the initial analysis of the creamer—and spilled coffee, which Henry's deputies apparently had also collected—was complete, but for now, we all knew she was getting off pretty easy.

It was entirely possible the judge—an old, cantankerous sort—had taken one look at her bright blonde hair and big blue eyes, and decided someone who looked like that couldn't possibly have committed such a heinous crime.

Once again, I had to scoop the bail money out of one of my accounts, but I knew that was no big deal. I'd get it back once Victoria went to trial…or sooner, I hoped. After all, the evidence seemed pretty circumstantial. For all any of us knew, the man hadn't been poisoned after all, and had actually dropped dead of a sudden heart attack or stroke. True, that quick glimpse I'd gotten of him seemed to show he was way too young for something like that to have happened, but otherwise healthy-looking people passed all the time from those same causes.

We'd just have to wait for the report from the medical examiner.

Archie—once he'd gotten past the initial shock of discovering his lady love had been accused of first-degree murder—looked as though he wanted to roast both Calvin and me alive. "How could you not have told me what was going on?" he demanded while we sat in the waiting area at Globe's police station and waited for the deputies to finish processing Victoria's paperwork. "I deserved to know!"

"Victoria made us promise not to tell you," I said, which was only a slight embellishment of the truth. She hadn't exactly come out and said so, but it was pretty clear she'd been hoping to get the blackmailer handled so Archie wouldn't have to learn anything about him or his nefarious demands. "She didn't want you to get upset."

"Well, that worked out just perfectly, didn't it?" he shot back, his voice dripping with sarcasm.

All right, this whole thing had gone completely sideways, but obviously, having the man drop dead in Victoria's studio wasn't an outcome any of us had been expecting. "We'll get it worked out," Calvin said calmly. "Right now, the most important thing is to get Victoria sprung and then try to figure out what really happened."

Truer words had never been spoken. At the same time, I couldn't quite hold back a creeping sense of unease. In the past, I'd dived pretty much headfirst into the assorted murder investigations that had come my way, sure that I'd be able to solve them with the help of my Tarot cards and my intuition…and also, maybe with a little extra assistance in the form of my grandmother Ellen, who'd passed on decades ago but who sometimes appeared in my crystal ball to offer her own other-worldly advice.

Now, though, with my gift of seeing auras gone and a general uncertainty whether my gut instincts were at all accurate anymore, I wasn't sure how much help I would be.

What if I'd lost the ability to see through to the heart of a matter, to discover the secrets a murderer might have been hiding?

I really didn't want to answer that question. Especially now, when the person wrongly accused was one of my dearest friends, and Archie's one and only love.

The last thing I wanted was for either Archie or Calvin to guess how uneasy I currently felt. Although neither one of them had come right out and said it—and although Calvin would never put that kind of pressure on me when I was carrying his child—I could practically feel the unspoken assumption that I'd sail in and save the day, just as I had for both of them in the not-so-distant past.

Victoria appeared then, accompanied by

Loretta Stillman, the deputy who usually worked at the Globe P.D.'s reception desk and who'd probably been chosen for this duty because she was friendly and low-key. To my relief—and Archie's and Calvin's as well, I guessed—Victoria wasn't wearing handcuffs, and actually appeared to have survived the brief ordeal with her usual aplomb.

"I'm fine," she told Archie in response to his urgent question, and smiled as he bent to kiss her and take her hands in his. "This is all just a misunderstanding. Or at least, I'm not surprised Chief Lewis arrested me, but I'm sure they'll drop the charges once they really start investigating the case."

A sunny view of the situation, but I understood why she'd want to look at it that way. If Henry Lewis—and the judge—really thought she was capable of such a crime, I doubted they would have given her such a low bail amount, or even allowed her to post bail at all. No, she'd still be cooling her high heels in a jail cell, just like poor Josie had last November, when Henry Lewis was convinced she'd slipped that arsenic into Pastor Galloway's backstage cup of coffee.

"Let's get you home," Archie said, and Victoria stared up at him as if he'd just suggested that they go hot-air ballooning.

"I'm not going home," she protested. "I've got a mountain of work to do."

At once, his jaw set. "You can't seriously be thinking of going back to the studio."

"Why not?" she said.

"Because a man just died there."

Victoria disentangled her fingers from his. "And that's why I have to act normal," she told him. "I have to act like I'm not guilty and everything is proceeding as if this is a perfectly typical day. If nothing else, I've got a ton of work to get through before the wedding, especially since I'm going to be gone for ten days afterward."

A small silence followed that pronouncement. I could almost see Archie turning various counterarguments over in his head, wondering if any of them would be persuasive enough to convince Victoria that going back to her office right after a supposed crime had been committed there would be a terrible look.

"Maybe you should work from home today," I said gently. "You have an office there, too, right?"

She nodded, expression dubious.

"Yes, that would be much better," Archie said at once. "Just give yourself a little space."

"I suppose so," she began, then paused. "It's not like I have any other meetings today, so it's okay for me to be at the house. But I can't stay away from my office indefinitely."

"You won't have to," I promised her. A sudden thought came to me, and I added, "I'll go through and cleanse the space so there aren't any negative energies left behind. Then I think it will be safe for you to go back to work."

A hopeful light shone in Victoria's clear blue eyes. "You'd do that?"

"Of course," I assured her. "Let's go to your office and pack up the stuff you need to work from home today, and then I'll handle cleansing the place. It'll be in much better shape for you to go back tomorrow."

And that was why the four of us headed over to Victoria's studio space—Calvin had already contacted his deputies to let them know he'd be late—and packed up her things and walked her back to her car. Archie offered to drive Calvin to get his police-issue SUV from our house once he got Victoria settled at their own place, and I finally headed back into Once in a Blue Moon nearly two hours after I'd left it.

"I'm so sorry about that," I told Melanie, who wore an expression of understandable curiosity on her face. "Something came up."

"Is everything all right?" she asked. "I heard sirens, and then there were a bunch of deputies outside. A little later, I thought I heard something happening in the lobby, but I was with a customer and couldn't check to see what was really going on."

There didn't seem to be much point in trying to hide what had gone down in Victoria's studio a few hours earlier—I knew the news would be all over town soon enough—so I didn't bother to lie, although I didn't think Melanie needed to know all the nitty-gritty details of the blackmailer's unexpected death.

"Victoria—the woman who owns the design studio upstairs—was meeting with someone, and he died," I said. My assistant's eyes widened, but I figured I should do what I could to forestall the inevitable questions and added, "What you probably heard in the lobby was the EMTs taking him out to their ambulance in the parking lot."

"Oh, my God," Melanie said, looking almost dazed by my revelation. "How awful."

Yes, it was extremely awful…but until we had more details, I didn't see the point in saying anything else on the subject. "It was," I replied. "That's why Victoria's going to work from home today. And I need to go upstairs and cleanse the space."

"'Cleanse'?" Melanie repeated, now looking dubious. "Shouldn't she hire cleaners for that?"

I did my best to hold back a smile. After all, my new assistant didn't know me very well, and even though I ran a New Age shop, that didn't necessarily mean she'd assumed that I subscribed to pagan beliefs.

"A spiritual cleansing," I explained. "I need to grab a few supplies, but it shouldn't take me much more than fifteen or twenty minutes. Can you hold down the fort for just a little while longer?"

"For as long as you need," Melanie said stoutly.

"Thank you," I said, and meant it. Not one word of complaint about being left alone in the shop for hours, even though this was only her third day on the job. Well, we were still in our honeymoon period, and I supposed she thought she needed to continue making a good impression on me.

It didn't take long to gather up a smudge stick and a couple of pieces of palo santo. There were other ways to clear an area than using rituals that some people thought appropriated Native American ways, but since Calvin had told me I should do what worked best for me—and since the smudge sticks I sold in my store were actually made by his fellow San Ramon Apache—I thought what I was doing should be all right.

I wouldn't be lying if I said I wasn't utterly thrilled about having to go into the studio by myself...the same key opened both our businesses, so there'd been no need for me to ask to borrow Victoria's...but I made myself mount the stairs, anyway. It never felt good to be in a place where someone had died unexpectedly, even though I hadn't gotten a sense that the blackmailer's ghost lingered in the fateful spot.

Then again, with my powers checked as they were by the child growing in my womb, would I have been able to feel the man's ghostly presence even if he was there?

That was a question I preferred not to answer.

Instead, I walked steadily up the stairs and into the studio. The deputies who'd investigated the crime scene hadn't taken very long, so there wasn't any yellow police tape barring my way, nothing except the knot of worry growing ever tighter in my midsection.

What if there really was a ghost lurking in Victoria's studio?

Then you'll talk to him, I scolded myself. *Stop being such a baby. It's not like this is your first rodeo.*

That was for sure. I'd had Danny Ortega's ghost as my almost constant companion while I tried to solve his murder almost two years ago now, and I'd also interacted multiple times with Alice Bigelow, the sad specter who'd hung around the Victorian mansion my parents had bought not too long after my arrival in Globe. Alice was gone, reunited with her lover in the afterlife, so the house was now blessedly ghost-free.

At any rate, I definitely couldn't claim that I had no experience dealing with the recently—or not so recently—deceased. However, I kind of doubted the specter of the blackmailer would be anywhere near as affable as Danny Ortega had been. Globe High School's former principal had been the kind of guy who wasn't fazed by much… not even by being dead.

I unlocked the door to the studio and let myself in. It felt strange to be here alone; Victoria had invited me in to see the place after the remodel was complete, and I'd popped in multiple times since then, but there had never been any reason for me to be there by myself.

There was also a sort of odd dissonance in seeing what the place looked like now and yet still recalling what it had been like back when I lived here. In a way, that shadowy overlay was its own ghost, a specter of the months I'd spent in the apartment…the window where I'd let Archie in from the balcony on my very first day here, the place where my dining room table had once been located, where Calvin had proposed to me on a snowy December evening not so long ago.

As best I could, I pushed all those memories away. Yes, it felt a little sad to be here, the melancholy wistfulness in my heart not so dissimilar from the same emotion I might experience when I came across an old photo of my younger self or a once-beloved dress that now needed to be donated to charity, but I had a job to do.

Victoria had kept the original wood floors and only sanded and re-stained them a lighter color, so cleaning up the spilled coffee had been an easy enough task for the deputies who'd bagged the evidence and cleared the scene. All the same, I was careful to skirt that part of the floor as I went over to the conference table so I could set down the smudge stick, abalone shell, and pieces of palo santo I was carrying.

Then I took in a breath and closed my eyes, doing my best to open myself up to the vibrations of the space. It all felt curiously neutral, as though nothing untoward had ever happened here…as if a man hadn't died in this very spot only a few hours earlier.

Well, that had to be good, right? At least, it didn't appear as if his spirit was lingering in the studio.

Or maybe I simply wasn't sensing anything because the baby was blocking any signals I might be receiving from the universe.

That idea didn't appeal at all, and I pushed it to the back of my mind as best I could.

But even if every scrap of psychic power I possessed was currently out of commission, that still shouldn't stop me from lighting the smudge stick and doing my best to send out as many good vibes as possible so the space would be workable for Victoria again. True, she hadn't seemed too worried about coming back to the studio. Despite that, it just seemed better for her to start over fresh when she returned tomorrow.

I'd brought along a lighter with the rest of my smudging supplies, so I lit the sage stick and let it flare for a moment before I blew on it gently to snuff the flame and have it smolder in the dried herbs. A faint trail of smoke emerged from the end of the little bundle, telling me it was ready to do its work.

After moving away from the table, I went to all corners of the room, letting the purifying smoke fill the space as I murmured the words of a cleansing charm under my breath.

Once that was done, I made a small paste of salt and spring water and dabbed it in all the corners and above the window and door—I had to go on my tiptoes to do that, but luckily didn't have to stop the ritual to search for a step stool—then headed into the kitchen and washed off my hands.

Was it enough?

I moved to the center of the space and stood there for a long moment, holding myself absolutely still, doing my best to reach out and see if anything had changed.

The space felt utterly calm. The only sound I

could hear was the faint hum of the air condi-tioner, and I made a mental note to turn it off before I left so Victoria wouldn't have to pay for energy she wasn't even using.

Problem was, everything had seemed fairly serene here even before I performed my smudging ritual, so I really couldn't say whether it had had any effect at all.

"Are you here?" I asked the room. My voice sounded odd to me, almost strained, although I told myself that was probably just because I didn't make a habit of talking out loud when I was alone.

No reply...not that I'd really expected one. Whoever that man had been, it seemed to me he'd decided he didn't have any reason to hang around this plane of existence.

And even though I should have been reassured by that, I still couldn't help feeling just a little disappointed. If nothing else, he might have been able to provide me with the information I needed in order to find out who had killed him.

Because I knew it sure as hell hadn't been Victoria Parrish.

But it looked as though the blackmailer had moved on, and that meant I needed to do the same thing.

Even if I had absolutely no idea what I should do next.

7

Private Eyes

ANY HOPES THAT I'D HAVE A COMPLETELY uneventful rest of my day were dashed when Josie Woodrow swept into the shop a little before noon and announced, "I just heard!"

I didn't bother to ask what she'd heard, or where. Gossip ran through our small town like a wildfire through dry brush, and Josie was generally at the nexus of Globe's neighborhood network. Also, I knew she loved Victoria like the daughter she'd never had, and therefore would have her ears pricked up especially high for any news that involved one of our most recent transplants.

All I could do was thank the Goddess that I'd let Melanie leave for lunch a little early, and so she'd wandered over to Cloud Coffee to get herself something to eat. Not that Josie and I would discuss anything that wasn't fit for my assistant's ears, but since Globe's mayor wasn't exactly the most discreet person in the world, it was just better that the two of us were alone in the shop.

"It's awful, isn't it?" I said, figuring I might as well get ahead of the conversation. "Victoria's a little shaken up, but she's doing okay. She's working from home today."

"I would think so," Josie replied. "Honestly, I'm not sure if I could ever go back to a place where something like that happened."

"Well, Victoria has sunk a lot of money into fixing up the studio," I said, which was the simple truth. I might have given her the place free and clear, but I knew she'd spent a decent chunk remodeling the apartment and creating the lobby area at the back of the building so people could either walk up the stairs to her studio or come through the new glass doors that led into the rear of Once in a Blue Moon. I'd offered to go halfsies on that part of the project, but she'd insisted on covering it all herself, saying the setup had been her idea and that she didn't want me to pitch in.

Because although Victoria looked like all sweetness and light on the surface, I knew there wasn't much that would budge her once she had her mind set on a matter. Typical Taurus, really, and I thanked the universe—not for the first time —that Archie's one true love had also been astrologically compatible with him. I could only imagine what a mess it might have been if she'd been a hot-headed Aries or a moody Cancer, rather than a fellow Earth sign.

"True," Josie allowed. "Still, I'm glad she's taking some time to work from home." A pause, and then she added, "And I assume you're going to help her get all this cleared up."

I'd kind of been wondering how long it would take for Josie to ask if I was going to step in and use my unusual set of skills to exonerate our friend. "I'm looking into it," I said vaguely, which was about all I could commit to right then. Although Josie wasn't really on board with all the woo-woo stuff, she also couldn't deny that I had a better track record when it came to this sort of thing than our local police chief.

Of course, that had been when I had full possession of all my not-so-mainstream talents... not that I planned to mention my misgivings on that subject to Josie. She was already clearly worried about Victoria, and telling her I wasn't sure I'd be able to help in any material way this time would only make her fear the worst.

Then again, I should have known Josie would see right through my off-hand reply.

"'Looking into it'?" she repeated, russet brows drawing together. She had flaming red hair that I doubted was natural, and she always leaned into the warm tones when autumn came around. Today, she wore a brown pantsuit with a rhinestone pumpkin brooch on one lapel, even though Halloween was still weeks away and one would have thought it was still way too warm to be wearing any layers.

Then again, Josie always had seemed impervious to heat, while these days, I felt as if I was roasting most of the time no matter what I wore. With my internal thermostat so haywire, I could only be very, very grateful that I'd be at my biggest in the depths of winter.

"I went up and smudged the studio," I explained. "I wanted to see if there was any trace of the man who died there, but I couldn't sense anything. His spirit has obviously moved on."

"Hmm," Josie responded, which could have meant just about anything. While she probably would have liked to pretend I had no ability to commune with the spirits, my success in removing the Bigelow mansion's ghost in the nick of time right before my wedding had proved otherwise. Then she went on, her tone turning brisk, "You know that Victoria's wedding is only a week from tomorrow."

While I wanted to say, "must have slipped my mind," I knew Josie wouldn't be happy to hear me being so flip about such an important occasion. All the same, I couldn't quite ignore the way she'd referred to it as "Victoria's wedding," as though Archie had very little to do with any of it.

Then again, Josie and Archie maintained an armed neutrality at best. Two strong personalities clashing, I supposed, although I had a feeling some of Josie's animosity had to do with the way Archie always managed to deftly evade any questions she might pose on the subject of his past… and the way she would then try to pry that same information out of me.

I always just said that I didn't know all that much, either, because my father had never been a part of my life while I was growing up, and I'd only contacted that side of the family after I was an adult. The story I always put forth was that Archie and I had hit it off at a party for one of my younger half-sisters during one of my infrequent visits to California, and he'd been entranced by the idea of getting out of the L.A. rat race and moving someplace where the pace of life was a lot slower.

No one else appeared to have much of a problem with that narrative, but Josie seemed determined to poke holes in it. She possessed very keen instincts about people—a talent I guessed she'd developed through all her years working in the real estate industry—and it seemed she could tell there was something a little off about my story. I had a feeling the only reason she hadn't really tried to grill me more about Archie was that Victoria was clearly besotted with him, and therefore, he must have plenty of sterling qualities… even if Josie might not see them.

"Yes, I'm perfectly aware of their wedding date," I said, knowing that a faint edge had crept into my tone. "But Victoria's out on bail, so it shouldn't really affect any of her plans."

Except for our girls' spa day in Gilbert, that is. The judge had said she needed to stay in town, and she hadn't protested, even though she must have known, just as I did, that we had a full day booked at the same spa we'd all gone to before my own wedding.

Well, there were worse things to worry about other than missing out on a mani/pedi. I'd make a few calls and see if I could get us into one of the nail salons here in town. It wouldn't be as high-end an experience, but the nail technicians here were perfectly competent, and it should all turn out just fine. Luckily, the hair and makeup artists had already planned to travel here for the wedding prep, so the only true casualty of this current mess was our fun day in Gilbert.

And there was also the little problem of Victoria and Archie's honeymoon in Sonoma and Napa. If the actual killer didn't present himself before then, those plans would be canceled as well.

Don't borrow trouble, I told myself. *You've still got a week.*

Right then, seven days didn't seem nearly long enough to get all this figured out.

"What if the judge revokes bail?" Josie said darkly, and I frowned.

"Why in the world would he do that?" I countered. "Victoria's a model citizen, and she's going to abide by the rules he gave her. Yes, she might have to postpone her honeymoon, but we'll figure out a way to reschedule it if necessary. The really important thing is that she and Archie get married, right?"

And I sent Josie a very direct look, challenging her to argue with me on that point.

She must have gotten the message, because she glanced away, saying, "Yes, of course. I'm just worried."

So am I, I thought, although I kept that sentiment to myself. "Right now, the most important thing is for us to provide a united front in showing support for the two of them. So let's keep our chins up, okay?"

"Okay," Josie said, sounding uncharacteristically meek, although that could have been the bells on the shop's front door jingling as it opened.

Melanie appeared then, holding a to-go cup of latte in one hand and a paper bag—presumably containing a sandwich—in the other. I straightened, saying, "Josie, this is Melanie Knowles, my new assistant. She's training right now so she can take over when I go on leave next year."

Josie put on one of her brisk smiles and extended a hand. "Very nice to meet you, Melanie," she said. "I'm Josie Woodrow, the mayor."

My assistant looked a little surprised that the store's latest visitor was someone so high-profile, but she gamely set the bag containing her sandwich down on the counter and shook Josie's proffered one. "It's very nice to meet you, too."

"Well, I won't keep you," Josie said, addressing those words to me. "Just keep me posted if there are any developments."

And she tilted her head at both of us and sailed out, leaving a faint drift of Chanel No. 5 in her wake.

"'Developments'?" Melanie echoed, now looking puzzled.

"Oh, we were just getting caught up about what happened in Victoria's studio this morning," I said hastily. "Josie doesn't like to miss out on any of the town gossip."

This explanation seemed sufficient, because Melanie didn't ask any further questions, but simply nodded and took her cup of coffee and sandwich with her back to the stockroom. I had a small table and two chairs set up back there for the times when I wanted to eat quietly alone, and it seemed my assistant wished to do that same thing. Maybe Cloud Coffee had been crowded and there hadn't been anywhere available to sit, or maybe she'd simply needed some time alone.

Whatever the reason, I was glad I was on my own in the shop for now.

I'd been purposely vague about what had happened upstairs, for obvious reasons, and yet I knew that eventually, Melanie would hear the whole truth about the situation, that Victoria was currently the primary suspect in her visitor's murder. All the same, I hadn't wanted to volunteer that information, and was currently just glad that Josie's and my conversation had been pretty much over by the time my assistant came back from her trip to Cloud Coffee.

A more pressing issue was that Josie obviously expected me to come striding in and save the day, and I honestly didn't know whether I was even capable of doing such a thing at the moment. I was all too aware of time weighing down on me, the depressing knowledge that I had a scant seven days to miraculously come up with both a perpetrator and a motive in Globe's latest murder.

Well, I couldn't do much about it right now. I had a shift to finish, and about all I could hope was that sooner rather than later, I'd have more information to work with.

———

"Jeffrey Sellers," Calvin told me over dinner that night, and I blinked at him.

"Excuse me?"

"Jeffrey Sellers is the name of the man who died in Victoria's studio this morning," my husband replied. "Ever heard of him?"

I shook my head. "Should I?"

"It sounds like he was a member of the ball-room-dance community in Phoenix," Calvin replied. "Which would explain why that black-mail letter Archie got had a Phoenix postmark."

I set down my fork so I could reach for the glass of water that sat on my right. "How did you hear about this?"

A corner of his mouth quirked. "Oh, I've got my sources in Henry's department. Let's just say that some of them seem to think you have a better chance of solving this crime than their boss does, so I'm getting fed some of the pertinent details."

"How…clandestine," I remarked.

The lift at the corner of my husband's mouth turned into an outright grin. "Well, I'll admit that it's helpful. Anyway, the interesting thing to me is that Jeffrey Sellers was a private investigator when he wasn't dancing the tango."

That piece of information made me sit up a little straighter. "So...you think this Jeffrey Sellers person found out something about Archie, and that's why he decided to dabble in a little blackmail to line his pockets?"

"It seems that way on the surface," Calvin replied. "Of course, there isn't much to go on right now, other than the guy's name. But even that small piece seems to line up with what all of us already suspected."

"Do Archie and Victoria know about this?" I asked next.

"Yes, I called Archie to let him know what I'd found out so far. He thanked me for the information, but he didn't seem too happy about it."

Probably not. After all, Archie was a very smart man and had probably made the same mental calculations I just had, namely, that the cover story and fake documents he'd been using to start his new life here hadn't been quite as convincing as he'd hoped they would be.

I tried to reassure myself that the dead man was a private investigator, the sort of person who'd been trained to look for discrepancies in people's stories, and that until now, no one seemed to have harbored any suspicions that Archie was anything more than he claimed to be. In fact, Archie had even been arrested for murder only a few months earlier, and those same documents had passed muster with the Scottsdale P.D.

"It's okay," Calvin said quietly, as though guessing at my thoughts. "Archie's been living this new life for more than a year now, and no one's raised any red flags. I'm pretty sure he's still safe."

"For now," I responded. I hated to be such a Negative Nellie, but I also knew we had to face the worst-case scenarios head-on so we'd be ready in case things went even more south than they already had. "What if the blackmailer had an accomplice, someone who also knows all about Archie?"

My husband's mouth tightened, and he was silent for a moment as he reached for his own glass of water and took a sip. Right then, he had the look of a man who wished it was something stronger, and I couldn't say I blamed him. I wanted the child I carried more than anything else...but I also would have killed for a nice glass of merlot right about then.

"If that were the case," Calvin said, "then you'd think Sellers' accomplice would have come looking for him. Have you noticed any strangers hanging around your shop or Archie's dance studio, anyone who looked as if they shouldn't be there?"

"No," I answered at once. "It was kind of

quiet for a Friday, so that made it easy to keep track of who was coming and going. I honestly didn't see anyone go near the studio at all, which I suppose makes sense. Archie would have called anyone who had a class and told them it was canceled."

Although Calvin had been his usual calm, reassuring self during this conversation, I could still see the way he relaxed slightly at my reply, how it was obvious to me that he was very, very glad I'd had such an ordinary afternoon. While I was also happy to realize that no suspicious characters had been hanging around the vicinity of my store, I also had to believe that anyone allied with the blackmailer probably would have gone out of their way to escape notice.

Or it could simply be that the blackmailer had been working alone. That made a lot more sense, simply because it meant he wouldn't have had to share his ill-gotten gains with anyone.

"That's good," Calvin said. "And when I go to the station tomorrow, I'll see what else I can find out about Jeffrey Sellers. Archie said the name seemed familiar but that he didn't remember having any direct contact with the guy, which doesn't surprise me too much. A lot of people enter those tournaments, and if Sellers was in a different division from Archie and Victoria, then there isn't any reason for them to have known each other."

My husband's comment made a lot of sense. I'd competed in one tournament while trying to track down Brad Masters' killer, but even that brief exposure had told me the novices had little contact with the open amateurs and pros, just like the people who took part in the country-western portions of the competition didn't have any reason to hang with those who specialized in Latin or ballroom dance.

Exactly why Jeffrey Sellers had decided to go after Archie, I didn't know. Had he smelled a rat for some time, had thought it seemed fishy for someone to appear out of nowhere and attain pro status in only a year?

That seemed the most likely explanation. However, it still didn't tell us exactly what Jeffrey Sellers had known, and when he'd discovered that information.

And whether or not anyone else was involved with his schemes.

But because I knew we wouldn't be able to solve those mysteries tonight, I only told Calvin, "I'm interested to hear what you find out."

He nodded, but his expression turned grim again as he said, "You still need to be careful. No one seems to have any idea how the murderer could have slipped something toxic into that creamer, which means we don't know how they gained access to Victoria's studio. I'd advise bringing in bottled water to drink and keeping a strict eye on it until we get this figured out."

Oh, hell. I hadn't even thought of that, but I usually brought in a container from home with water in it, and casually left it out sitting out on the counter. If I turned my back, anything might happen.

And I really didn't want to mention how I wasn't always as careful about turning on the alarm as I should have been. Victoria and I had agreed that the last one out was the person in charge of making sure the alarm was activated, but there had been several times when she'd left early, and it had completely slipped my mind. No one had ever tried to break in, so at the time I'd figured it was no harm, no foul. Now, though, I wondered if I'd inadvertently given the murderer the opportunity to slip into the building and do their dirty work.

Of course, everything would have been locked up, and there didn't seem to have been any signs of forced entry, but maybe a skilled lock-picker wouldn't have left any traces behind.

I hesitated, wondered if I should mention any of this to Calvin, then decided it wouldn't change anything. If I'd forgotten to lock up, that would have been one thing, but I was always very careful about making sure the building was secured before I got into my car and left for the evening. No, better to let it go for now. I resolved to be much more careful about the alarm system in the future, then guided our conversation toward other, safer topics.

Maybe I should have been working harder on solving this mystery, but right then, I was tired, and only wanted to pretend everything was normal…

…and hope like hell that inspiration would strike me the next day.

8

Where There's a Will

I DIDN'T KNOW ABOUT INSPIRATION, BUT I realized the next morning—after I'd woken up earlier than usual and knew I'd be dressed and ready for the day long before I needed to be at the shop—that I might as well put my unexpected extra time to some good use.

In this case, that meant breaking out my Tarot cards and seeing if they could help point me in the direction I needed to go.

Calvin had already left for work; he was doing as many Saturday shifts as possible before I went on maternity leave, just so there wouldn't be too much resentment about him working mostly weekdays once I was home with the baby. Normally, I would have been glad for the extra peace and quiet—it wasn't that my husband bothered me when I was in my office, but sometimes simply the presence of an additional person in the house could disrupt my readings—but right then, I didn't know for sure whether the cards could help me at all, or whether it would turn out I was just as blocked from receiving their messages as I seemed to be from everything else psychic or spiritual.

Still, I lit some incense and the tea lights that sat on my altar, and breathed in and out for a moment, doing my best to let the calming perfume of the white sage incense settle into my soul and bring me the clarity I so desperately needed. Sadie followed me into the room and settled herself in her bed, but she was always around when I performed my readings, and having a dog in the space was nothing like having a person there.

Two separate questions tumbled through my mind, both of them important, both of them inextricably linked.

What made Jeffrey Sellers decide to blackmail Archie? And who really killed him?

I shuffled the cards and shuffled them…and shuffled them. Usually, I'd experience a little twinge or tingle when I got to the right card, a gentle sign from the universe that it was time to stop shuffling and make a pull at that particular moment, but I didn't seem to be receiving any such signals today.

Even though I could already feel my neck beginning to tense, I told myself it was all right, that this wasn't the first time when it appeared the universe wasn't quite ready to communicate with me.

True enough, but after losing my auras, this was not what I wanted to be dealing with right now.

Any chance you could tell your "medicine" to take a hike for a bit? I asked the baby, and set down the cards I held so I could place a hand against my belly. It was just starting to swell in earnest, although a casual onlooker still probably wouldn't have guessed I was pregnant, might have only thought I needed to lay off the pizza and sweets for a while.

No response, of course, because it was too early for the baby to really start kicking, but I had to hope he or she was listening.

I picked up the cards again and began shuffling them, telling myself I wasn't going to wait for a sign, but was just going to keep mixing them together for at least another minute. Then I could go ahead with my card pull.

Which I did, taking three cards and laying them down on my altar, on top of the pretty autumn-hued cloth I used at this time of year. In a few weeks, I'd switch it out for my Halloween one, with its ravens and black roses, but for now, the backs of my Everyday Witch cards stared up at me from a backdrop of fall leaves.

There was my old friend, the Ten of Swords, with the hapless witch lying face down with all ten of those blades sticking right out of her back.

So…betrayal of some sort, which didn't even require a signal from the universe to be clear. Generally, getting poisoned was a pretty good sign someone had betrayed you.

If, as I'd speculated earlier, Jeffrey Sellers had been poisoned at all, and hadn't merely been struck down by an untimely heart attack or stroke.

The second card was the Moon. It was often a trickier one to interpret, mostly because it dealt with things hidden, sometimes illusion or deception. Again, this didn't seem too out of place when we were dealing with a murder, because right now, the truth of who might be at fault was as obscured as the moon on a cloudy night.

The third card was the Fool, reversed. A lot of the time, I didn't do reversals in my readings, but in this case, I knew the card was upside down for a reason. The upright Fool meant new beginnings, faith in the universe—symbolized by the literal "leap of faith" the person depicted on the card was making—but reversed, it could mean chaos, folly, lack of judgment.

Had Jeffrey Sellers made a colossal error in judgment?

Well, most people would probably say that deciding to blackmail an innocent man was a terrible error in judgment, but I had to believe something else was going on here. Exactly what, I didn't know yet, but as I scooped up the cards, I couldn't help feeling just a bit relieved. I hadn't gotten a clear sign that these were the cards I'd been meant to pull, but at the same time, it had been a consistent enough reading, one that seemed to tell me I was still getting signals from the universe, even if I was a bit slow about receiving those messages.

Considering how much I'd been doubting myself lately, I'd take it.

Because it was a warm, friendly Saturday in early October, the shop was busier than it had been the preceding few days. We had several tour buses stop by, along with a lot of foot traffic, including Joyce Lewis, Henry's wife. She dropped off a box of her wonderful scented candles and looked as though she wanted to chat, but we were just busy enough that it wasn't really feasible. I introduced her to Melanie, thanked her for the candles, and said I hoped we'd be able to talk the following week.

Otherwise, not much of note occurred, although Calvin texted me early in the afternoon to tell me he'd learned a few things about Jeffrey Sellers and that we could talk more when we both got home that evening. I was a little disappointed we couldn't talk then, although I told myself it would be better to wait to have that conversation when we were alone. It wasn't that I didn't trust Melanie, but I certainly didn't know her well enough yet to take her into my confidence.

And Victoria came by in the late afternoon, looking a bit strained. Because Melanie had just stepped out to take her afternoon break, I didn't have to worry about her overhearing anything the two of us said.

"Everything okay?" I asked, and Victoria gave a brief nod.

"Sure," she replied, and I raised an eyebrow, knowing that she wasn't telling me the complete story.

"Well, I had to talk the developers down," she said. "They weren't too thrilled to hear about my arrest."

"They didn't take you off the project, did they?" I responded, alarmed. She'd been so proud of landing such a big client so early in her designing career, and I knew she'd be devastated if she was fired because of this mess.

"No," Victoria said. "They just wanted to voice their concerns that my 'legal troubles' might prevent me from fulfilling my contract. I assured them everything was fine and that I wouldn't have any problems getting all the designs finalized on the timeline we'd agreed upon." She paused there and let out a small breath. "And I know that's the truth, because my lawyer told me he doubted we'd be going to trial for at least a couple of months, and the model homes are supposed to open the second week of November, but...."

"But you didn't need the extra stress right now," I finished for her.

"Exactly," she said, a tired smile just barely lifting the corners of her mouth. "It's okay, though. I'm just going to keep my head down and get as much done as I can before next weekend." Another pause, and she added, "We're going to have to cancel our spa day, though."

"I figured," I responded. "But it's okay. I'll make some calls. I'm sure I can find someone to squeeze us in somewhere."

And I would...even if it meant offering extra-large tips to any salon who shuffled their schedule around or stayed open late to accommodate Victoria's wedding party.

"You don't have to do that—" she began, but I only shook my head.

"What else is a matron of honor for?" I asked, then went on before she could reply, "You haven't given me many duties, so this is the least I can do."

"Thanks," she said, the expression of gratitude on her face so obvious that I knew she was being completely truthful. "I've always told myself I can handle whatever comes my way, but this—"

"This is a big old pile of crap," I told her. "We all know that. So if there's anything Hazel or I can do to lighten the load, you just let me know."

"I will. Now, though, I need to grab a few things I forgot to pick up yesterday."

"That's fine," I said. "I completely cleansed the studio, and there's absolutely no sign of a ghost, so spend as much time up there as you need."

Victoria was used enough to me that my airy remark about ghosts and cleansing didn't even earn me a blink. "Good to know," she said easily. "Especially since I really need to be back here on Monday. But you have a good rest of your day— and thanks again, Selena."

"That's what I'm here for," I said with a smile.

This time, the smile she sent me in return was a lot less weary, and I hoped my words of encouragement had helped, if even a little. She headed out the back door just as Melanie returned with a cup of iced tea. Good thing I was paying her so well, or she would've blown half her salary on keeping up with her caffeine fix at Cloud Coffee.

"Was that Victoria?" she asked, clearly having spotted my friend's departing form as she headed into the rear lobby.

"Yes, she needed to pick up a few things from her office," I replied.

"And is she doing okay?"

"Mostly," I said. "I'm glad she's only here to get some work and then go back home, though. I have to think it'll help for her to have a few days away from the office to give her some mental space."

"I suppose," Melanie said, and now she looked a little dubious.

"'You suppose'?" I repeated.

At once, she looked abashed. "Sorry," she said. "It's just that I heard people talking at the coffee shop, and—"

Of course, people were gossiping. That's what they seemed to do best around here. Still, I tried to keep myself from sounding too stern as I replied, "Yes, a man died under suspicious circumstances in Victoria's studio, so the police chief felt he needed to arrest her. But she did nothing wrong, and I know she'll be exonerated soon enough."

That comment was my signal that I didn't

want to discuss the subject any further, and Melanie took the hint, telling me she was going to stock the incense display, if it was all right with me. That was just fine, as far as I was concerned; the shop had been busy so far today, but it wasn't anything I couldn't have handled on my own.

My assistant headed back to the stockroom to retrieve the incense packets, and I allowed myself a sigh. I'd definitely sounded confident when I'd said I had no doubt the charges against Victoria would be dropped soon...but I didn't feel that way inside. No, not at all.

Exactly a week from now, she was supposed to marry Archie. The conditions of her bail would allow her to do so, but what kind of wedding would it be with that sword of Damocles hanging over her head?

I had to figure this out.

I just had to.

The day had been warm enough that Calvin offered to barbecue our dinner, and I was immediately on board with his plan. Even kitchen witches liked to get the night off occasionally.

He grilled skewers of chicken and veggies, and I summoned the energy to do some rice in the Instant Pot to go along with them. Sadie was thrilled with these preparations, mostly because she knew the skewers would provide plenty of opportunity to be fed some choice morsels during dinner.

After Calvin had poured some San Pellegrino for the two of us, he said, "So…Jeffrey Sellers."

"What did you find out?" I asked.

"He definitely was a private detective, just as we'd already guessed," my husband replied, then took a bite of grilled chicken. "He was thirty-five, and had been practicing for about seven years."

That seemed young to me to be a P.I., although I reminded myself that what you saw on TV and in the movies didn't necessarily match what was going on in the real world. "And the ballroom dancing?"

"He's been doing that for about four years," Calvin replied. "Still in the novice category, although he's competed in a couple of pro-am events. Sort of middle of the road, I guess—he's made it to third place a couple of times, but he definitely wasn't lighting up the competition scene the way Victoria and Archie have."

Which seemed like a perfect reason for him to be jealous of the two of them. "Partner?" I asked, and ate a mouthful of rice.

"He's had a couple," Calvin said. "Which isn't super strange, I guess—it sounds like people in the dance world change their partners all the time.

The woman he was currently dancing with is someone named Sara Tilden. She lives in Gilbert."

Which was nice and close to Globe…comparatively speaking. "Maybe I should go talk to her," I suggested, and Calvin's dark eyes narrowed.

"I'm not sure that's a very good idea," he told me. "Selena, you can't go around putting yourself in danger right now. I was never on board with the chances you take in the first place, and now…."

His words trailed off, but I got the point. It was one thing for me to decide whether or not a risk was acceptable when it was just my own safety I was putting on the line, but now that I was pregnant, I really needed to be doubly cautious.

"Are you saying this Sara Tilden person is a risk?" I inquired.

"Probably not," he said. "The little research I could do on her makes it seem as if she's an ordinary enough person. She's a respiratory therapist at Dignity Health in Gilbert, and she'd been dancing with Jeffrey Sellers for about eight months."

"Were they an item?"

One of Calvin's eyebrows lifted a fraction of an inch, but I just gazed back at him calmly. It really wasn't such a strange question to ask—from what I'd been able to tell, a lot of dancers seemed to develop physical relationships with their partners, although of course it wasn't a given.

"I don't know," he admitted. "If they were dating, it's not the sort of thing that would show up on a simple background check."

No, it wouldn't. If she'd been married to Jeffrey Sellers, that would have been one thing, but as it was....

"See, that's even more reason for me to go talk to her," I said. "I don't have to work tomorrow, and neither do you. We could go together. That would be safe enough, wouldn't it?"

A long pause as my husband eyed me, obviously trying to figure out whether this latest scheme would be better or worse than me going on my own. "Henry would skin me alive if he found out I was directly interfering with his investigation," Calvin said slowly.

"So, I'll go alone."

"No," he responded, an amused light in his dark eyes. "I'll drive you and wait in the car. And you'll call me at the first sign of trouble. Okay?"

The offer was honestly more than I'd expected. While there wasn't technically anything Henry could do to Calvin for interviewing someone who might or might not be connected to Jeffrey Sellers' death, at the same time, he could try his darnedest to make life miserable for both of us if he really wanted to. Just acting as my chauffeur and muscle might be enough to invite the police chief's ire, but clearly, concern for my safety—and the safety of our unborn child—outweighed any of those concerns.

"It's a deal," I said, and Calvin made an odd little twist of his mouth, as if he wasn't sure whether he should be relieved or worried that I'd agreed to his plan so quickly.

Honestly, I didn't think either of us had anything to worry about. Henry had probably already interviewed Sara Tilden, so there shouldn't be any reason for him to visit her after their initial conversation. No, Calvin and I could just skate over to Gilbert tomorrow when we thought it most likely that Sara would be at home, I'd ask her a few questions, and then we'd be back in Globe before anyone even noticed we'd briefly popped out of town.

Now I just had to hope she'd have something to say that would be worth the trip.

9

Dancing Queen

THAT SUNDAY WAS SO PICTURE-PERFECT, I almost wished Calvin and I could use it for a picnic or a nice, mellow hike. But we'd already decided that catching Sara Tilden at home around eleven was our best strategy, so I had to put that idea aside for now.

"We can have lunch at Zinburger, though," I told Calvin as he guided my Jeep Renegade down the gravel lane that led to the main road. Normally, we would have been driving his big Dodge Durango, but since it had the San Ramon tribal police's seal on the doors, it wasn't exactly inconspicuous.

He sent me an amused glance. "So that's what this is really about, huh? Are you having a craving for one of their Samburgers?"

"Maybe," I said primly. "I just don't see why

we can't mix business and pleasure, since we're driving all that way. Besides, on the off chance someone from Globe is also visiting Gilbert today and spies us, that'll give us a good excuse for being there."

Apparently, Calvin decided he couldn't really argue with my logic, because he only nodded as he maneuvered us onto the road and started driving west. It was not quite an hour and a half drive each way, so I settled myself against the back of the seat and tried to enjoy the novel experience of having my husband pilot a vehicle I usually drove.

There was never much traffic on that route, so we made good time and reached Gilbert's city limits at just a few minutes past eleven. Sara Tilden lived in a rented townhouse not too far from the cute downtown area—convenient for us, because that offered us some additional plausible deniability in case anyone we knew actually saw my vehicle and recognized it.

We pulled up to the curb, and Calvin rolled down his driver-side window and turned off the engine. "Ready?"

I nodded. To be honest, my heartbeat had sped up a little, because even though I'd been the one who'd insisted on this interview, it was still nerve-wracking to have to talk to a complete stranger about a murder. Would Sara be teary and heartbroken, or—like Joanna Greer, who'd lost her partner when Peter Tillis decided to hack him into little pieces and hide him in a trunk—would she be more matter-of-fact, mostly worried about finding a new dance partner so she wouldn't have to take too much time away from the competition circuit?

Only one way to find out, I supposed.

Hoping I looked more confident than I felt, I opened the car door and let myself out, then walked up the neat front path to Sara Tilden's blue-painted front door. I had to admit these townhouses were very cute, with their vaguely vintage architecture that matched Gilbert's restored downtown area, and I kind of hoped the friendliness of my surroundings might match the woman who lived in the home with that cheerful blue door.

I pushed the button for the doorbell, and a simple "ding-dong" rang from inside the house. A moment later, the door opened, and a woman who looked like she was probably in her late twenties or maybe early thirties stared out at me, clearly perplexed to find a complete stranger standing on her flowered welcome mat. She had dark blonde hair with some careful highlights, and eyes somewhere between blue and gray.

If she'd cried recently, I couldn't see any sign of it. No reddened eyelids, no puffs.

Was that a good or a bad thing?

"Can I help you?" she asked.

I'd already resolved to be truthful, hoping that would make Sara Tilden more inclined to confide in me. Maybe all this would get back to Henry, but I'd deal with that when I had to. "Hi," I said, and extended a hand. "My name is Selena Marx. I was wondering if I could talk to you about Jeffrey Sellers."

A shadow passed over her features, one I might have missed if I'd blinked. "Are you a cop?"

"No," I said, then took a breath. "I'm a friend of the woman who was arrested following his death. I know she had nothing to do with it, and I'm trying to clear her name."

This forthright approach appeared to take Sara aback for a second or two, because she blinked, then hesitated before saying, "I don't know if I can help you, but sure—come on in."

The first hurdle cleared. I couldn't exactly heave a sigh of relief…or turn toward the spot at the curb where Calvin waited in my Renegade so I could give him a thumb's up…so I just followed Sara inside her townhouse. It had a small foyer with a single white-painted table in it that held some cheerful yellow flowers in a bubble-glass vase, and was obviously fairly new, based on its cool, gray-toned neutral color scheme.

"We can sit in here," Sara told me, leading me into a small living room with an L-shaped sectional upholstered in white linen and a glass-topped round coffee table. "Can I get you anything to drink? Some water?"

"I'm fine," I said, which was only the truth. Calvin and I always filled go-cups with water from our filter in the fridge before we set out on any drive that was longer than just going to the local grocery store, so I definitely wasn't thirsty. "And thank you so much for taking the time to talk to me."

Sara made a small hitch of her shoulders. "Like I said, I'm not sure how much I can help."

As we both sat down, I said, "Really, anything might be valuable. I know my friend didn't do this, and I'm just trying to figure out who would."

"Oh, I know Victoria Parrish had nothing to do with Jeffrey's death," Sara told me. "I said the same thing to Chief Lewis. Pretty much everyone loves Victoria."

That revelation made me feel a little better. Not that I'd expected anything less; even so, I'd been worried there were dancers out there who were just as jealous of Victoria as Jeffrey Sellers had been of Archie.

"Can you think of anyone who might've had a grudge against Jeffrey?" I asked next, and again, Sara gave a faint shrug.

"Well, he was a private detective," she said. "I

know some of the stuff he dug up helped break up a couple of people's marriages."

"Anyone in particular?"

She shook her head. "Jeffrey didn't give me any details. It was just the sort of thing he liked to brag about."

I blinked. "He bragged about ruining people's marriages?"

Sara didn't answer at first, and instead looked over one shoulder, as though she halfway expected someone to be eavesdropping on us despite our obviously being alone in her townhouse. Apparently satisfied there would be no other witnesses to her next words, she said, "Just between you and me, he was kind of a jerk. I only partnered with him because I needed someone to dance with, and his former partner had dropped him for someone who was already dancing in the pro division, so he was available."

"So, you two weren't…?" I ventured delicately.

That insinuation earned me a vigorous shake of the head. "God, no," Sara replied at once. "We danced together, and that's it. I mean, I'm not saying we didn't go out for a drink after a competition every once in a while, that kind of thing, but there was nothing personal going on between us. Life is complicated enough, you know?"

I reflected that it definitely was. After making a murmur of assent, I said, "But you don't know anything specific about who might have considered Jeffrey an enemy?"

"Not really," Sara replied. "I have to admit I wasn't too surprised to hear that he'd been murdered, just because of the whole private-detective thing, but that's about it."

Maybe the information I needed was still locked up in his office, where I assumed he must have kept various client files. However, I doubted I'd be able to access any of it. Burglary really wasn't my thing.

Unless....

"Did Jeffrey have any family, someone in the area who might have a key to his office?"

At once, Sara shook her head. "No, he was a transplant from somewhere in the Midwest. Iowa, I think. But you don't need someone from his family to help you out with that. I've got a key."

About all I could do was blink at her again. "You do?"

"Yes, he gave it to me a couple of months ago when he was going to be out of town for a while and he needed me to come in and feed the fish."

Well, there was an unexpected stroke of luck. "He didn't ask for the key back?"

"No. I asked him about it, but he said it was probably better for me to have it, since I was his only real emergency contact in the area."

Although what I'd heard about Jeffrey Sellers

so far definitely made it sound as if he hadn't been the world's nicest guy, I still couldn't help experiencing a twinge of pity at hearing that revelation. Even though he'd apparently lived in the Phoenix area for years, he didn't have anyone he could trust beyond his current dance partner, no family, no close friends.

"Would you mind if I borrowed the key for a bit? I'll bring it back as soon as I'm done looking around his office," I said then, knowing even as I spoke that it was an awfully big ask.

Sara hesitated. Although she didn't quite bite her lip, I thought I saw her teeth catch on it for a second.

"He's got confidential stuff in there," she said, her tone reluctant in the extreme.

"I know," I replied. "And I would never go poking around in it if I wasn't trying to find something that could prove Victoria is innocent. I won't share what I find with anyone…unless I turn up something that seems to show someone else had a motive for killing Jeffrey."

A long, fraught moment passed. I had to force myself to sit there quietly, to wait until Sara had given herself the necessary time to wrestle with her conscience and decide whether to hand over the key.

Then she said quietly, "Give me a minute."

She got up from her spot on the couch and

headed toward the stairs. I could hear her moving around in one of the rooms on the second story, and the sound of a drawer shutting. The townhouse was very nice, but its walls were paper-thin compared to the thick adobe I was used to in the home I shared with Calvin.

Then she came back down to the living room and extended a plastic fob with a brass key hanging on it. Stamped on the fob was the legend, *Sellers Investigations…Prompt, Thorough, and Discreet.*

I didn't know how discreet it was to announce your private investigation business on a key fob that you handed out to clients, but whatever. The important thing was that Sara was actually giving me the key to Jeffrey Sellers' office.

"His office is in Mesa, on 2^(nd) Avenue," she said. "It's about fifteen minutes from here."

Perfect. Calvin and I could grab an early lunch to fortify ourselves, and then we could head over to Mesa to see what we could find.

"I'll be as quick as I can," I told Sara. "Are you going anywhere today?"

Her mouth quirked. "No, Sunday is laundry day around here. I was just about to put a load in when you rang the doorbell."

Even better. At least now I wouldn't have to worry about making Sara hang around the house while Calvin and I got something to eat and then went to investigate Jeffrey Sellers' office.

"Then I'll be back with the key in no more than a couple of hours," I promised.

"Sure," she said, then added, "Could you feed the fish while you're there? I took care of them yesterday, but…."

"Of course," I said, again experiencing one of those sad little pangs. The fish could not understand that the person who'd faithfully fed them every day was now gone forever. I supposed Sara —or maybe Jeffrey's family, since I assumed they'd need to fly in from Iowa at some point to handle the aftermath of his death—would have to find a new home for the fish and their tank, but for now, I was happy to take care of them.

Maybe that would make me feel a little less guilty about pawing through people's private business in my hunt to find Jeffrey Sellers' real killer.

I thanked Sara again for her help, then headed back out to the car, where Calvin had been sitting with the driver-side window rolled down so it wouldn't be too obvious to anyone watching from the house. The day was definitely too warm for him to have sat there with zero airflow, and since he hadn't known how long I was going to be inside Sara's townhouse, keeping the Renegade's engine running wouldn't have been a very good idea.

"Any luck?" he asked as I opened the passenger door and climbed in.

"Maybe," I replied, and brandished the key Sara had given me. "This goes to Jeffrey's office in Mesa. I'm hoping we can find something in his files there that might point us to the actual killer."

Just the smallest tightening of my husband's lips, telling me he wasn't too enthused about the idea of going through people's private records. However, he must have weighed the somewhat dubious morality of performing such a search against the very real danger of Victoria getting convicted of a crime she didn't commit, and decided there was only one real choice here.

"All right," he said. "What's the address?"

"Lunch first," I responded. "I can already feel my blood sugar crashing."

He didn't argue, of course. We might have been on a mission, but his wife and the child she was carrying came first.

Luckily, it wasn't quite noon yet, so we were able to slide right into a table at Zinburger, beating the weekend lunch crowds. We already knew what we wanted, so we ordered our beverages and food simultaneously, and were in and out of the restaurant in record time.

"Okay," Calvin said after we were back in my compact SUV. "Now you can tell me that address."

I gave it to him, and he programmed it into the Renegade's navigation system before pulling out of the parking lot and onto Gilbert's main drag, heading north so we could intersect Main Street and then drop down onto 2nd Avenue.

The drive only took us about fifteen minutes, and soon enough, we were pulling into the strip mall where Jeffrey Sellers' office was located. It was a shabby place, probably built in the late 1960s or early '70s, occupied by a nail salon and a CPA, with several of the storefronts vacant, their front windows mostly obscured by large signs advertising affordable office space.

Judging by the very faint lift of my husband's brows, I could tell he wasn't too impressed by the place. Neither was I, but our surroundings weren't important.

No, the really important thing was what we might find in Jeffrey Sellers' files…assuming, of course, that he didn't have everything locked down on a computer whose password we didn't know and probably wouldn't be able to hack.

However, if getting into his computer had been a possibility, I had to assume Sara would have said something, since she'd been to Jeffrey's office to feed his fish.

A little sign next to the door said the office was protected by A-1 Security Services, and I shot a nervous glance at Calvin. "What if there's an alarm?"

"Then wouldn't Sara have said something to you about it?" he replied.

I had to hope so. Quite possibly, the sign was there for show and nothing else. "And if we do set off an alarm?"

He didn't look too worried. "Then I'll show the responding officers my I.D. and let them know I'm here on official business. Not that they'd be real police—an outfit like this is the kind that uses rent-a-cops exclusively."

There might have been just the slightest hint of scorn in his tone. I brushed it aside, partly because I'd encountered that attitude from him before and knew it was pretty typical, and partly because it wasn't worth worrying about when we had more important things to do.

No alarm shrilled as I unlocked the door and opened it, telling me that the sign about the security service definitely was for show and nothing more. Maybe once upon a time, Jeffrey Sellers actually had retained their services, but had discontinued them when the cost got to be too much.

Either way, it looked like we were getting inside his office with no trouble.

Calvin followed me in, flicking on the lights as he went. They showed a space that was basically a small ten by ten box, with an old-style metal desk in approximately the center of the room and two worn swivel chairs in front of it. Against one wall were three metal file cabinets, while the other was dominated by the aforementioned fish tank, an impressively large affair sitting on top of a faux-wood cabinet.

"You check the files, and I'll take care of the fish," he said, moving toward the cabinet.

I wasn't sure if that was the best plan—would I even know what I was looking at if I did find something incriminating in one of those files?—but then I realized Calvin probably thought it was better for me to thumb through them, maybe hoping that my intuition would kick in and I'd recognize a key piece of information as soon as I stumbled over it.

Fingers crossed.

The file cabinets were putty-colored, dinged and scratched. I got the impression that they hadn't been bought new, but picked up at a yard sale or maybe a going-out-of-business kind of event.

Obviously, Jeffrey Sellers had done whatever he could to save money. No wonder he'd thought blackmailing Archie was a good way to pad his bank accounts.

The file cabinets were labeled with the letters of the alphabet, so I decided I might as well start with "A." However, thumbing through those files didn't give me any tingles, didn't seem to have anything in them beyond receipts and a few intake forms, maybe from people who'd thought about hiring Jeffrey to handle their personal problems but had decided against it.

As I made my way through the alphabet, I found more of the same, and did my best to fight back against the discouragement I could feel building somewhere in the pit of my stomach. "There's really nothing here," I told Calvin after I'd made my way to the "M"s and had still come up with bupkis.

He came over and gave my tense shoulders a gentle rub. Just the sensation of those strong fingers against my tight muscles made me feel better. Not all the way better, because I was starting to think this trip had been a complete waste of time, but having Calvin next to me always got me thinking there was no problem without a solution, even if I couldn't yet guess what that solution might be.

"You're not all the way through the alphabet," he said. "But how about I start at the end and work back, and we can meet somewhere around 'R'?"

"That would mean you'd need to get down on your hands and knees to get to the stuff at the end," I said. "Maybe I should do that part."

"Nope," he replied cheerfully. "I'm not having my pregnant wife crawling around on this crummy carpet. I'll do it."

Well, I had to admit the carpet had definitely seen better days. It was that close-pile stuff that seemed to be confined to commercial use, and maybe once had been dark beige but was now a muddy sand color.

"If it'll make you feel better."

He shot me a grin and lowered himself to the floor. Good thing he was wearing jeans and not his khaki uniform slacks, or the Goddess only knows what kind of stains he might have picked up down there.

I continued to "N" and started rifling through the files. Once again, I found nothing noteworthy, and progressed on to "O."

"Wait a minute," Calvin said, and I paused, fingers resting on a manila file.

"Did you find something?" I asked.

"Maybe."

He pulled out a manila file folder identical to the one I was currently touching, then pushed himself up to his feet—no easy task for someone who was almost six and a half feet tall. Then he handed the folder to me.

"Take a look at this," he said.

Inside the folder was a set of paperwork I quickly identified as final divorce papers, with an accompanying child and spousal support decree.

"Jeffrey Sellers had a child?" I said, flabbergasted. Everything Sara had just told me about him made it seem as if he didn't have any real family at all.

"Sure looks that way," Calvin said. The genial light I'd seen in his dark eyes only a moment earlier had disappeared, and he now looked uncharacteristically grim. "And there's this."

He pulled out a sheaf of papers, one that seemed to be a stack of letters from his ex's lawyer, getting progressively more strident as time went on and the unpaid support bills piled up.

"So…he skipped out on them," I said, and Calvin nodded.

"Looks that way," he replied. "Maybe he thought escaping to Arizona would be enough to keep them from coming after him."

"You think his ex-wife might have killed him in retaliation?" I asked, knowing I needed to ask the question, even though I hated the very idea of it.

Calvin's shoulders lifted. "I don't know. It wouldn't be the first time something like this has happened. Maybe his ex felt as if she had no other choice."

My head was spinning. I stepped away from the file cabinet and sat down in one of the shabby swivel chairs, hoping that would combat the dizziness. "But how would Jeffrey Sellers' ex even know he was trying to blackmail Archie and Victoria, let alone gain access to Victoria's studio so she could poison the creamer?"

Or the coffee itself, I supposed. I still hadn't heard anything about exactly what had killed the man, so I didn't know what means had been used to deliver the toxin.

Calvin came over and sat in the other chair, turning it so he faced me directly. "It's hard to say. Maybe his ex confronted him, and he told her he had a plan to get his hands on some money, fast. That could explain how she would have known where he was."

I supposed that theory made some sense, but…. "If she was expecting a payout from Jeffrey, why kill him?"

It seemed Calvin had already thought this through, because he replied at once, "It's possible she wanted to take all the money for herself, or maybe she thought he was going to cheat her out of it, just like he'd cheated her out of years of child support."

None of this still felt exactly right, but because I didn't have any better theories, I just nodded.

"Anyway," my husband went on, "this paperwork has her full name—NancyAnne Nielsen—and her social, so it won't be too hard to track her down, find out where she is. I can get one of my deputies on it."

I didn't bother to protest that this technically wasn't his investigation, and if Henry Lewis found out that Calvin had been using his own officers to work on the problem, he might not be too thrilled about it. My husband was a grown man and a smart one, and he could do his own risk analysis of the situation and determine the best way to proceed.

"But let me take a quick look at the rest of the files, just so I can see if there's anything else that might be promising," he said. "You rest."

That sounded like a great idea. The dizzy sensation had passed, but I didn't much like the idea of hunching over those files and thumbing through them. I was just fine with letting Calvin handle that task.

However, he didn't find anything more, nothing that would have told us someone else had a grudge against Jeffrey Sellers, so we locked up and headed outside. Walking out the door felt awfully conspicuous, and I halfway expected Henry Lewis to pounce and demand to know what we were up to.

Obviously, that didn't happen. No, Henry was over sixty miles away, probably enjoying his afternoon off by watching a football game, or maybe heading up to Payson to go fishing. He certainly could have had no idea that Calvin and I were pursuing our own investigation here in Mesa.

One that seemed to have hit pay dirt, although we didn't have any concrete evidence that NancyAnne Nielsen had had anything at all to do with her ex-husband's death. Plenty of motive, true, but....

We climbed into our car and headed back to Sara's house so we could return the key.

"Should we tell her?" I asked after we were back on the road.

"About Jeffrey's ex and child?"

I nodded.

"For now, I wouldn't," my husband replied, then flickered a glance in my direction before returning his attention to the busy streets around us. "Unless they were romantically involved or something."

"They weren't," I replied, my tone emphatic.

"You're sure?"

"I'm sure," I said. Yes, I was just going on Sara's remarks on the subject, but if she'd been lying, she was awfully good at it. If my damn auras hadn't taken a powder, I might have been able to see hers and get a much better read on what she was really thinking and feeling, but for now, I'd just have to go on body language and her general demeanor to form an opinion.

Calvin didn't offer any protests, which relieved

me to no end. He knew I generally had good instincts about people even when their auras weren't involved, so there was no reason to believe Sara had pulled the wool over my eyes in this particular case.

Soon enough, we were parking in front of her townhouse. I got out and went to the front door, and rang the bell. A moment later, she appeared, expression curious.

"Did you find anything?" she asked.

"Not really," I replied, telling myself it was just a little white lie. "But we fed the fish and locked up. Do you know what's going to happen to them?"

"Oh, I'll keep going by and feeding them until one of us hears from his family," Sara said. "A couple of people in the dance community have already put together a GoFundMe to help cover funeral costs, that kind of thing, and if Jeffrey's family doesn't want to deal with the fish, I know a guy here in Gilbert who can probably take them."

That news was a relief. I hated the thought of the fish dying of neglect...or, possibly worse, getting flushed when someone decided they were too much trouble. At least it seemed as if Sara and her fellow members of the dance community were doing what they could to make the best of a bad situation.

"Thank you for doing that," I said. "And thanks for the key."

"But you didn't find anything," she said, and I allowed myself to shrug.

"I know. But at least we tried." I paused there, then sent her a smile I hoped looked genuine. "And we fed the fish."

She smiled back, an expression that also seemed a little forced, and I figured it was time to go. I waved goodbye and headed down the front walk to the spot where Calvin waited for me at the curb.

We'd uncovered one of Jeffrey Sellers' secrets.

I couldn't help wondering how many others he'd been hiding.

10

'Til Death Do Us

BECAUSE IT WAS A SUNDAY AND THEREFORE they were a little short-staffed at the San Ramon police station, Calvin said he'd bring up the subject of NancyAnne Nielsen with his deputy the next morning, since Ben Ironhorse, the one person employed by the tribal police who was a true genius with computers, would be there.

"I know it's a little bit of a delay," he said as he bent to kiss me on the cheek. "But I'll have Ben working on it first thing."

"It's fine," I replied, even though I wasn't sure exactly how "fine" any of this was. We'd headed into the living room when we got home so I could sit in my favorite armchair and put my feet up on the footstool there. Of course, I didn't get much of a chance to relax before Sadie came bounding up so she could settle herself in my lap, but that was all right. With the dog parked there and showing no signs of going anywhere else anytime soon, that meant Calvin would have to be the one to go into the kitchen and get me a drink of water, which of course he did as soon as I made the request.

He returned with the glass and handed it to me, saying, "That definitely wasn't a wasted trip, though, which is something. I have to admit, I was worried we might not find anything of any use."

"Me, too." I sipped the water gratefully; yes, I'd had water to drink in the car, but there was just something special about a fresh glass of ice water handed to you by your gorgeous, thoughtful husband. "But if I'd only talked to Sara, I wouldn't have learned much. It was a huge help being able to look at Jeffrey Sellers' files."

"That's for sure." Calvin paused there, his expression thoughtful. I was sure I wasn't the only one to notice there hadn't been a computer on the desk in Jeffrey's shabby little office. Had he used a laptop, bringing it back and forth from work?

That seemed like the most likely explanation, meaning the computer must still be in his house or apartment…assuming, of course, that Henry Lewis hadn't confiscated it as evidence. Maybe not; Jeffrey hadn't died at his home, and that meant Chief Lewis might not have had probable cause to search the place.

But even if the laptop wasn't tucked away in an evidence locker somewhere, it was still at Jeffrey Sellers' residence, which meant I couldn't easily gain access to it, either. I supposed I should just be glad that all the paperwork from the family court in Iowa had been just that—papers—and therefore he'd needed to store it somewhere.

So many questions crowded my mind—if NancyAnne Nielsen really had killed Jeffrey, was she still here in Arizona? Would she have left some kind of paper trail?—but I knew most, if not all, of them would probably be answered the next morning after Calvin got to work. The good thing was that he had to be on shift at 8 a.m., several hours before I was due at the shop. With any luck, he'd turn up the information then, and we'd be able to discuss it while I was here at home. Not that I didn't trust Melanie, but most of this stuff was private, and not the kind of thing I wanted to talk about when there was a possibility of her overhearing me.

Because I knew I'd just have to wait to see what happened next, I smiled up at Calvin and said, "So…what do you want for dinner?"

To my infinite relief, he called me around nine-fifteen the next morning. "Hey, hon," he said. "Ben was able to pull up some information."

A little shiver of excitement went through me. "What'd he find?"

I was sitting on the bed when Calvin had called and just about to slide into a pair of flats, meaning this was the perfect time to pause and hear what he had to say. From her spot at the foot of the bed, Sadie looked at me expectantly, as though she'd heard her master's voice coming through the tiny speaker of my iPhone.

"It looks like NancyAnne Nielsen is here in Arizona right now," he told me. "She flew in to Phoenix the middle of last week."

That little shiver of excitement turned into an outright surge. "So...she would have been here the day Jeffrey Sellers was murdered."

"Yes, she got here two days before." Calvin paused there, then added, "It looks as though she's staying at a hotel near the airport."

Which made sense, if she'd thought she would be confronting Jeffrey at his home or his business in Mesa. She probably hadn't bargained on having to drive all the way out to Globe to do the dirty deed.

If, of course, she'd killed him at all. Right now, it was impossible to know for sure.

"Is her daughter with her?" Somehow, the

thought of NancyAnne killing Jeffrey while she had their child in tow was even worse than the actual reality of his murder itself.

"It doesn't look that way," Calvin replied, and I let out a breath of relief. "That is, Ben says there was only a charge for one round-trip ticket on her credit card."

You'd have thought she would have paid cash for her airline ticket, considering that sort of transaction would have left a pretty obvious paper trail. Then again, even without those credit card receipts, there would still have been a record of her on the flight's manifest. Maybe it wasn't as big a deal as I'd originally thought.

"She probably left the child with relatives in Iowa," Calvin went on. "The little girl is pretty young, only around seven."

I did some quick mental math. If Nancy-Anne's daughter was only seven, then that meant she must have been born right before Jeffrey left Iowa and headed west toward greener pastures. That sounded like an awfully cold response to your child's birth, but it was entirely possible the marriage had been on the rocks before she was even born. I'd definitely heard that sad story more than once.

Including my own case, although at least my parents had only been dating, not married. Still, my biological father had definitely made himself scarce once I appeared on the scene.

And although I'd long ago come to terms with my father's absence in my life, telling myself this was just how things were supposed to work out and how I shouldn't be bitter about any of it, I had to admit that Jeffrey Sellers' abandonment of his daughter made me like him even less, if possible.

Honestly, if it weren't for the inescapable truth that finding his actual killer would exonerate Victoria, I doubted I'd go to so much effort trying to find out who was responsible for his death.

"And she hasn't checked out of her hotel?" I asked.

"No. Ben said the hotel reservation was from the fourth through the ninth, so she should still be there. Her flight home leaves at 2:20, so she'll probably be checking out right at eleven and then heading to the airport after that."

"We need to talk to her before she leaves, Calvin," I told him, hoping the urgency of my words was apparent even over the phone.

A breathy little sound that I guessed was a sigh. "I can't leave," he replied at once. "Jacob's wife went into labor this morning two weeks early, so we're short-staffed today."

Damn it. That is, I was happy for Jacob and

his wife, but we just couldn't let the opportunity to interview NancyAnne Nielsen slip past.

I blurted, "I'll go talk to her."

"Selena—"

I knew that warning tone and chose to ignore it. "Calvin, I've *got* to talk to her. Even if she isn't our suspect, she might be able to provide some valuable information about Jeffrey's enemies, that kind of thing."

"NancyAnne Nielsen and Jeffrey Sellers have been split up for years," my husband pointed out. "Do you really think she has any idea what was going on with his life here in Arizona?"

Maybe not. What I did know was that it felt as if the universe was sending me a clear signal. NancyAnne was still here, only an hour and a half away. I knew I could make it before checkout time if I got moving right now.

And I also got the feeling if we let her get on that plane and fly back to Iowa without even trying to talk to her, we might miss out on something extremely important.

"And you have to be at work, too," he reminded me. "You've only had Melanie working for you for a couple of days. Do you think it's fair to leave her alone like this?"

I only hesitated for a second. "Yes," I replied. "I mean, the whole point of hiring her was to have someone who could watch the store while I was on maternity leave. Besides, it's a Monday, and Mondays are usually dead at the shop. She'll be fine."

Calvin didn't reply immediately, which told me he still wasn't on board with the plan, but knew he couldn't outright forbid me to drive to Phoenix so I could talk to NancyAnne. "Be careful," he said after a long pause, his way of giving in gracefully.

"I will," I said.

"I'll call you if I learn anything else," he told me. "Love you."

"Love you more."

We ended the call there, and I hurriedly finished getting dressed. I knew I'd have to run to the shop to open up, because I hadn't given Melanie a key yet. It was on my list of things to do, but with all the craziness that had been going on lately, getting one had completely slipped my mind.

It was fine, though. I'd swing by the store, open things up, and then be on my way. At least it wouldn't be too much of a detour, five minutes out of my day at the very most.

Now I just had to hope NancyAnne would really be at her hotel and hadn't headed to the airport early.

In which case, I'd just have to track her down there.

"I'm so sorry to spring this on you," I told Melanie. "But I completely forgot that I needed to drive to Phoenix for some tests this morning."

Her hazel eyes flared with something like alarm. "Is everything okay?"

"Oh, it's fine," I assured her. "It's just that there are a few things my local doctor can't do, so I need to go see a specialist. I'm hoping I'll be back around one so you can take a late lunch, but if I'm not, you can just lock up and put the 'be back at' sign in the window and go get yourself something. People are used to the shop being closed at odd hours, so it won't be a problem."

"I can have something delivered—" she began, but I only smiled.

"Delivery around here can be a little spotty," I said, which was the simple truth. Travis Cox, Globe's one and only Uber/Lyft driver, also supplemented his income by driving for Door-Dash. He meant well, but he got distracted, and your food would get delivered cold…or not at all…more often than not. "It's really better to just close up and go get yourself something. But I'm hoping I'll be back by the time you need to take a lunch break."

"Okay," Melanie replied. "I'll hold down the fort. Have a safe drive!"

"I will," I said automatically.

As I headed out back so I could get into my car, though, I couldn't help thinking that the hundred-mile trip ahead of me was the least of my worries.

It had been quite a while since I'd been anywhere near the airport; the last time I'd traveled out of state was to handle all the legal matters following Lucien Dumond's death and the huge mountain of cash he'd left me. I'd made half-hearted promises to my mother that I would visit her in California, but my new life in Globe had turned out to be much busier than I'd expected, and I just never seemed to make the time.

I probably would have felt more guilty about the situation if she and Tom, her husband, hadn't owned a positively gorgeous Victorian home right here in my adopted hometown, and it really made more sense for them to come to Arizona rather than vice versa.

Because even though I'd never come right out and say such a thing to my mother, I knew I'd be perfectly happy if I never set foot in L.A. again.

Traffic was thick, which I'd kind of expected but found annoying after more than two years of living in Globe and getting used to its much slower pace. Still, I was able to fight my way to the parking garage at the hotel and leave my Renegade there…even as I winced at the hourly rates they were charging.

No one ever had to pay for parking in Globe, that was for sure.

The information Calvin had given me said that NancyAnne Nielsen was staying in room 810, up on the eighth floor. It had been a long time since I'd been up quite that high, and I had to take a couple of deep breaths as the elevator climbed to my destination. No, it wasn't exactly that I was afraid of heights…but I much preferred to be a lot closer to the ground.

Room 810 was located roughly in the middle of the long row of doors down the hallway. A man and woman pushing a cart laden with luggage moved past me as I hesitated outside the door, and I waited until they were safely inside the elevator before I lifted my hand to knock.

So many precious seconds passed that I wondered if I really had struck out here, and that NancyAnne actually had gone to the airport early, even though her flight wouldn't be leaving until after two.

But then the hotel room's door opened, and a woman who looked like she was probably in her mid-thirties stared out at me. She was pretty in a thin, strained kind of way, with hair somewhere between brown and blonde and unusual light brown eyes, almost amber. "You're not Jeffrey," she declared in accusing tones, and I stared back at her in shock.

Was it possible she didn't know?

"No, I'm not," I said. "My name is Selena. But I'd like to talk to you about him, if that's okay."

Her eyes narrowed. "Are you his girlfriend?"

"God, no," I replied at once, knowing I sounded properly horrified. "I'm married."

She hesitated, then said, "Why do you want to talk to me about him?"

"Several reasons," I said, and added, "But I really think it would be better if you would let me inside so we can speak privately."

Another of those pauses, during which her gaze slid past me toward the corridor outside her room, as if she halfway expected me to have an accomplice lurking somewhere nearby. But then she appeared to decide I was alone and probably safe enough, because she stepped aside and told me, "Come on in."

It wasn't the most gracious invitation I'd ever received, but that was okay. I went past her into the room, noted that it had two queen beds— only one of which appeared to have been slept in —and looked neat and tidy, with her luggage stored in the closet and no obvious belongings apparent anywhere except a paperback Nora

Roberts novel lying face down on the table that was situated between the two beds.

"You can sit down over there, if you want," NancyAnne told me, inclining her head toward the small table and pair of chairs that sat near the window. "I don't have much time, though. Checkout is in fifteen minutes."

"That's okay," I replied. "I'll try to make this fast."

I settled myself in the chair closest to me while she watched, eyes slightly narrowed. I didn't miss how her gaze went to the rings on my left hand, the engraved band and matching engagement ring with its brilliant round-cut white sapphire. It wasn't the world's most traditional wedding set, but it appeared to convince Nancy-Anne that I'd been telling her the truth about being married, because she nodded slightly to herself before she came over and sat in the unoccupied seat.

The last thing I'd expected to do during this visit was break the news to Jeffrey's ex-wife that he was dead, but I supposed I should have prepared myself for that eventuality. I wasn't exactly privy to everything Henry was working on regarding the investigation, and yet it seemed to me that he had no idea NancyAnne—or her child—even existed.

No, they seemed to be part of a past Jeffrey

Sellers had been all too happy to leave behind him in Iowa.

"I hate to have to tell you this," I said, once she'd settled herself in her chair. "But Jeffrey died three days ago."

At once, her amazing tea-colored eyes widened. Was it those eyes that had first attracted him?

"He *what?*"

"He…passed…under suspicious circumstances," I explained. "Right now, the police think a very good friend of mine had something to do with it, but I know she's innocent. I'm trying to learn as much as I can about him to see if I can figure out who's actually responsible."

As soon as I mentioned Victoria—even though I hadn't stated her name—resentment flared in NancyAnne's expression. "Was your friend his girlfriend?"

"No, no," I said quickly, even as I wondered what NancyAnne's hangup about Jeffrey Sellers' love life might be. Had he cheated on her?

Or did she still have feelings for him, even though it was obvious he hadn't treated her—or their daughter—well at all?

"My friend is engaged," I went on, knowing I needed to clarify the situation as quickly as possible. "She's actually getting married on Saturday. No, we have every reason to believe

Jeffrey was trying to blackmail her and her fiancé."

Immediately, NancyAnne's face twisted, and I thought I glimpsed pure rage in her tea-colored eyes. "That bastard," she whispered.

I stared back at her. "Has he done this kind of thing before?"

She shook her head. "No. Or at least, not that I know of, but we haven't exactly been in close contact these past few years." She pulled in a breath, and I noticed how her mouth tightened, as though she knew she had some damaging things to say about her ex but didn't much care. "I came to Arizona because I couldn't think of what else to do. He ignored the court orders, and since he worked for himself and kept changing banks, there wasn't any proper way to garnish his wages, either. Things got so bad that I had to move back in with my parents."

"I'm sorry," I murmured, even as I thought that karma definitely had caught up with Mr. Sellers in the worst way possible.

NancyAnne gave a little shake of her head, as if to show she really didn't want my sympathy. "Anyway, I came here so I could confront him in person. I guess I was hoping I could pressure him to give me something, even if it was just a couple thousand dollars so I'd have enough money for a deposit on an apartment or whatever."

"And did you see him?" I asked, even as I wondered where she'd gotten the money for the plane ticket and the hotel room. Her parents? Possibly. I could see how they might have dipped into their savings to pay for the trip if it meant financial freedom for their daughter.

"Yes," she replied promptly. "Last Wednesday, the same day I got to Phoenix. I gave myself plenty of time here, since I didn't know how long it was going to take to try to make him do the right thing. He told me he was going to have a lot of money soon and that I just needed to hang tight."

With those words, the situation began to fall into place. Jeffrey had seen NancyAnne, and either guilt or just plain worry that she'd show up on his doorstep whenever she wanted had made him realize he needed to get some money, fast. Clearly, he'd already hatched the plan to blackmail Archie and Victoria, since the first threatening letter had appeared several days before Jeffrey's ex had arrived in Phoenix, but her presence had definitely added some extra urgency to the mix. That was probably why he'd gone to see Victoria in person, hoping she would hand over the money then and there. I didn't know how much he was planning to extract from my friends, but clearly, he'd expected enough that it would get his ex-wife off his back for a while.

NancyAnne must have been making those same mental calculations, because she said, "That's where he was going to get the money, wasn't he? From your friends?"

"I think so," I replied. "But he didn't have a chance to demand the money before he died."

"She shot him?"

I stared at her, startled by the suggestion, then said, "No. It looks like Jeffrey was poisoned, but I haven't heard exactly with what. Something fast-acting, something I think was in the coffee my friend served him."

"But she didn't do it."

NancyAnne's expression was almost blank, as if she was doing her best to hide her skepticism at my protests of my friend's innocence. I suppose on the surface, the scenario seemed sort of implausible...at least, if you didn't know Victoria the way I did.

"No, she didn't," I said calmly. "Someone must have put the poison in the creamer she used, or maybe the coffee itself."

"Jeffrey always needed his creamer," Nancy-Anne responded in almost musing tones. "If someone doctored the stuff, they'd have to know that about him."

That theory made sense. Of course, it didn't explain who would have been able to get into Victoria's studio and add the poison—whatever it was—to the creamer. As far as I knew, the only people who had keys to the place were Victoria and Archie...and me...because although she had a cleaning crew who came in to tidy the studio once a week, she always arrived early on those days to let them in. They definitely didn't have a key of their own.

And even if they did, I couldn't think of a single reason why anyone on Victoria's cleaning crew would want to put poison in her creamer, let alone specifically place it there to kill Jeffrey Sellers.

"Do you know of anyone who would want him dead?" I asked next, wanting to wince at how awful those words sounded, even while I also knew I couldn't dance around the question.

NancyAnne's mouth twisted. "You mean, besides me?"

About all I could do was nod.

"I've been out of his life for seven years," she said. "I really don't know what was going on with him. The only reason I even knew where his apartment was located is because I hired a private detective of my own to track him down."

Excitement surged through me. "You have the address to his apartment?"

She sent me a dubious look. "What, are you going to break in and rifle through his stuff or something?"

"Maybe," I admitted. "I might find a clue there that could help me find out who really killed him. The reason I could track you down was because he had your divorce papers and child support claims in a file in his office."

That admission made her eyes narrow again. "You're sure you're not a cop?"

"I'm definitely not a cop," I said, trying not to smile. "But I've actually solved a lot of murders… more than the local police, to be honest. And this one is personal, because it involves my friends."

NancyAnne was silent then, apparently doing her best to absorb everything I'd just told her. "His place is in Mesa," she said. "Let me get the address."

She rose from her chair and opened a drawer in the hotel room's dresser, pulled out a plain brown purse, and retrieved her phone from inside. It was an iPhone several generations older than mine, its screen cracked, as if she hadn't had the funds to either have it repaired or buy a new one.

Well, of course she didn't, I thought. *With the way Jeffrey Sellers stiffed her on child support, she probably had to use every last dime on rent and food.*

And even that apparently hadn't been enough, since she'd had to move back in with her parents.

"Nineteen-fifteen South Harris Street, apartment number 122," she announced, obviously reading something from her contacts list.

"Just a sec," I said, and dug my own phone out of my purse. I couldn't ignore the way she almost glared at my iPhone, obviously the latest model and something I could only have bought within the last couple of months. Well, while I could sympathize with her current situation—it hadn't been so long ago that I'd also had to keep my phone on life support for as long as possible— it wasn't as though I'd had anything to do with it.

No, her current financial difficulties had everything to do with the man who'd dropped dead in Victoria's studio last week.

I wrote down the address and said, "Thank you for that. I don't know if I'll find anything, but—"

"I don't want to know," NancyAnne said clearly. "Jeffrey is gone, and I spent all this money and time coming here for absolutely nothing. Knowing the truth isn't going to help me or my daughter."

Probably not. Still, I hated to leave things on such a depressing note, and ventured, "Maybe he had a will?"

She made a disgusted sound. "Even if he did —even if he had any assets worth passing on—do you really think that deadbeat would have left a single goddamn dime for his daughter?"

His track record of paying child support...or not paying it, more to the point...indicated he probably wouldn't have. Still, people sometimes made capricious decisions when it came to determining where their money would go after their deaths.

After all, I wouldn't have my current financial security if it weren't for Lucien Dumond deciding to leave all his money to me rather than to a family member, or even one of the more dedicated acolytes in his organization.

"It's really hard to say," I replied gently. "But I think it's worth pursuing...if you don't mind."

NancyAnne gave a bitter laugh. "Go right ahead and break into his apartment. I don't care. Now that I know he's gone, I'm going to get out of this hellhole and go back where I belong."

A little part of me bristled at the "hellhole" comment, but I didn't bother to try defending my adopted home state to the woman. She'd just suffered an awful shock, not because she still had feelings for Jeffrey...or at least, I didn't think she did...but because he'd promised her money and she now had zero chance of collecting any of it.

If she ever had. For all I knew, he'd had some trick up his sleeve to make it look as though he was paying her off, but instead was doing exactly the opposite, like giving her a fake cashier's check or something.

"I'm sorry," I said again. Empty words, but I knew I needed to respond somehow.

I got up from my chair, my purse draped over one arm. NancyAnne didn't move.

"I guess you can see yourself out," she told me.

I nodded, then hurried away from her, back out into the corridor, and hurried toward the elevators.

That hadn't gone as planned, not at all. But at least I'd gotten one vital piece of information.

Now I knew where Jeffrey Sellers had been living at the time he'd died, and maybe—just maybe—if I were really lucky, I'd find something useful there.

Fingers crossed.

11

Inside Job

I WAS ALL TOO AWARE OF HOW TIME WAS passing, and how I really should be getting back to Globe so I wouldn't leave Melanie alone at the store for too long. But there was no way I'd go home without stopping at Jeffrey's apartment in Mesa first.

After all, it was right on my route home.

Well, mostly. It turned out the apartment complex where he'd been living was a good ten minutes off the highway, not exactly optimal. But it wouldn't have made any sense to go back to Globe and then turn around and come here after my workday at Once in a Blue Moon was over with.

The complex reminded me a lot of the strip mall where Jeffrey Sellers' office had been located, in that it was probably decades old and in desperate need of updating. I still hadn't formulated any clear plan about getting inside, although I'd concocted a half-baked story about going out with him on a date and leaving my phone inside his place. The chances of getting a sympathetic building manager to let me in were probably zero, but I had to start somewhere.

However, after I located his apartment—situated on the ground floor, to my relief—I noticed something very odd when I put my hand on the doorknob.

It wasn't locked.

I blinked and looked around. No one seemed to be out and about, which made sense in the middle of a workday. It was almost noon, telling me people possibly could have started to come home for lunch, but right now, the complex seemed pretty much deserted.

Well, fortune favored the bold.

I went into the apartment, then immediately closed the door behind me. As my eyes adjusted to the dimness within—a huge contrast to the almost painfully bright blue day just on the other side of the door—one thought went through my mind.

What a dump.

The furniture all looked as though it had come from garage sales or maybe Facebook freebie swap groups, and none of it matched. Also, the air had a faintly sour, stale smell, as if something inside the refrigerator or the pantry had gone bad during Jeffrey's absence. And unfortunately, he was never coming back to clean it up.

My stomach turned over, and I told myself I needed to get it together, that I was well past the morning sickness that had given me some grief during the third month of my pregnancy. True, just because I'd had a relatively trouble-free past couple of weeks, it didn't mean the nausea might not decide to return.

Especially when I was being assailed by some pretty severe stank.

I breathed in through my mouth and reminded myself that the faster I looked around the apartment, the quicker I could be out of there and on my way.

Luckily, the place wasn't very big, just a small living room with a dinky dining area next to the equally postage-stamp-size kitchen. I figured I'd leave that for last, and headed over to a short hallway that opened on a bathroom on one side and a bedroom on the other. The bathroom didn't look as if it had been cleaned since Jeffrey Sellers moved in, and sported a nice collection of bristles on the cultured-marble countertop. A quick look in the tiny vanity told me there wasn't anything under there except a half-used pack of generic toilet paper and a shaving kit.

Likewise, the bedroom didn't seem to contain anything of note—the bed was rumpled, with the comforter pulled up toward the wall behind the pillows in a half-hearted attempt to make it look as if it had been made, the bedside table didn't have any drawers for me to even peek into, and a quick look inside the highboy dresser told me there wasn't anything interesting there beyond socks and underwear and a few spare pairs of jeans and messily folded T-shirts.

And although I was holding out high hopes for the closet, there was nothing to find in there, either, just a couple of pairs of khakis and one slightly wrinkled plaid jacket.

Well, damn it.

Absolutely no sign of a laptop or other computer. Unless Jeffrey had hidden it under the sink or something, it must have been stashed someplace else.

Frowning, I went into the kitchen, doing my best to continue breathing through my mouth. A quick glance inside the refrigerator told me the likely source of the sour smell was a couple of containers of ancient Chinese takeout, and I closed the door quickly and turned back toward the living room, hands on my hips and what I guessed was a fearsome frown wrinkling my brow.

Had Jeffrey Sellers been one of those Luddites

who didn't believe in having any kind of computer, or was I missing something?

Maybe it was in his car, I thought then. *He had to have driven to Globe, so he must have left his car somewhere in town.*

That thought cheered me a little. Unless you had a derelict vehicle taking up space in your front yard or left it blocking a neighbor's driveway, the Globe P.D. rarely wasted its time writing parking tickets. It was entirely possible that Jeffrey's car was still sitting on a side street somewhere, collecting dust. Maybe at some point someone would call it in as abandoned and it would get towed, but that process could take up to a month or more.

Which meant I might have been looking in entirely the wrong place.

"Damn it," I muttered under my breath.

Time to get back to Globe…but also to call Sara Tilden to ask her if she knew what kind of car Jeffrey drove. I had to imagine she'd know, just because they'd probably carpooled to dance tournaments from time to time.

However, I'd only taken a few steps across the shabby living room when the front door suddenly swung inward. Steely gray eyes met mine.

"Selena Marx," Henry Lewis said. "Why am I not surprised?"

"I didn't break in," I told him after I recovered from my shock. "The door was unlocked when I got here."

One eyebrow lifted, but then Henry surprised me by saying, "I didn't think you had. I may not appreciate some of your methods, Ms. Marx, but breaking and entering seems a little beneath you."

My anxious stomach unclenched a bit, even as I found myself very, very glad that Henry Lewis wasn't a mind reader. Otherwise, he would have seen that the only reason I hadn't resorted to picking the lock to let myself into the apartment was because I didn't know how.

"There's nothing here," I told him, figuring we might as well plow ahead. "I already checked the whole place."

He sent me a cool stare. "Maybe," he allowed. "But I'm sure you won't mind if I look around myself?"

"Go ahead," I said magnanimously. "But I think I'm going to wait outside. I can't take the smell in here anymore."

That might have been a gleam of amusement in his flinty eyes. "Probably a good idea. This shouldn't take me very long."

After delivering that comment, he walked into the bedroom, while I stepped outside. The warm breeze that stirred the oleanders planted next to the postage stamp of a front porch felt like heaven after the stinky confines of the apartment, and I breathed in deeply, glad that my stomach already felt like it was beginning to settle down.

While I waited, I pulled out my phone to check on the time. Just past one, so I knew there was no way in hell I was going to make it to Globe before two, and maybe not even by then. I could only hope that Melanie had taken my advice and had closed up shop so she could grab some lunch.

Henry emerged from the apartment a few minutes after that, wearing his characteristically expressionless expression. "What were you looking for?" he asked.

"A computer or a laptop," I replied. "There was nothing at his office."

The line between the police chief's brows deepened at that reply, telling me he wasn't too thrilled to learn I'd already visited Jeffrey Sellers' office. "When did you go there?"

"Yesterday," I replied, even as I made a mental vow not to mention that Calvin had been with me. I added, "And no, I didn't break in. Jeffrey Sellers' dance partner gave me the key."

"Sara Tilden?" Henry asked, and I nodded.

He didn't look too happy with that revelation, but probably decided there wasn't much he could do about it. Jeffrey had given Sara the key, and with him gone, it was her choice as to what she wanted to do with it.

"But you didn't find anything," he commented.

"Well, I didn't find a laptop," I said, then paused. Should I even mention NancyAnne Nielsen?

For all I knew, Henry had already learned about her existence, probably from court records. Being a cop gave you access to all sorts of information an ordinary citizen wouldn't be able to lay their hands on, so it was entirely possible that what I thought was a big secret was a nothing-burger to him.

"But you found something else," Henry said.

Not for the first time, I cursed my complete lack of any kind of poker face. You'd think after investigating all these murders and encountering all sorts of crazy stuff, I'd be a little better at keeping my thoughts to myself.

"Jeffrey Sellers' ex-wife," I replied.

Henry's gaze flickered ever so slightly, but that was his only reaction. "NancyAnne Nielsen?"

"You knew about her?"

"Of course," he said, then went on, his tone just a little too smug, "Their marriage and divorce is a matter of public record, so her information came up when we were doing a standard background check on him. But she's in Iowa, so we didn't consider her a suspect."

Ha. At least there was something I knew and Henry didn't. "Well, actually," I said, "she's here."

Shock registered on his blunt features before he could completely hide it. "In Mesa?" he demanded.

"No, in Phoenix," I said. "She's staying in a hotel at the airport. Or at least, she was. She had a two o'clock flight today, so she's probably waiting somewhere at the airport. But she's definitely checked out of the hotel by now."

"Damn it." He pulled in a breath, the look on his face telling me he wasn't happy with himself for allowing even that brief outburst in my presence. "When I talked to her, she told me she was at home in Davenport. How long was she here?"

I hesitated. Revealing that NancyAnne had been in the Phoenix area for the greater part of a week would only get Henry thinking she'd had ample opportunity to slip that poison into the creamer.

Well, except for the part where she had known nothing about the blackmail plan or Victoria.

Unless she had.

What if she and Jeffrey had been working together, and she'd decided to kill him so she could keep all the blackmail money herself?

The thought of the two of them working as a

team didn't seem very likely, though. And what was the point of killing him before he'd even gotten the money from Victoria?

Maybe she miscalculated, I thought then. *Maybe she'd thought the poison wouldn't act as quickly, and he wouldn't die until after he'd gotten the money.*

"I think around the middle of last week," I said, after I realized Henry would only have to do the same thing Calvin's deputy had done to get all the information he needed about NancyAnne's itinerary, so there didn't seem to be much point in trying to hide it.

His eyes narrowed again, and I could tell he was doing the same mental math I'd performed only an hour or so earlier. "Well, it sounds as though I need to have another chat with Ms. Nielsen," he said. "Might be time to remind her that making false statements to an officer of the law is a crime in this country."

"Don't do that," I blurted, and he shot me an annoyed look.

"Why not?"

"Because she's just had a shock," I replied. "She didn't know Jeffrey was dead until I told her. Also, she's got a small child at home, and is living with her parents because Jeffrey bailed on his child-support payments. But I suppose you already knew that."

Henry didn't reply right away, telling me I was right, and that he knew all about NancyAnne Nielsen's home situation. "Still," he said after a weighty pause, "even if she's innocent, she's not making a very good case for herself by lying to the police regarding her whereabouts."

I couldn't argue with that observation, so I settled for giving a tiny lift of my shoulders.

To my surprise, Henry seemed satisfied with that response, saying, "Well, there's nothing more either of us can do here, so I think it's a good idea if you head back to Globe, Selena. You have a store to run, after all."

No point in telling him I had an assistant managing the place for me in my absence, because I guessed his wife Joyce had already let him know about my new hire. Should I mention my theory that Jeffrey might have hidden his laptop in the trunk of his car?

Might as well, I told myself. *You might earn back a couple of brownie points.*

"Have you searched Jeffrey's car?" I blurted, and Henry Lewis sent me a look that could only be described as condescending.

"That was one of the first things we did," he said. "He left it parked a couple of blocks down from Victoria Parrish's studio, and we had it towed to the impound yard. There was nothing to find."

"No laptop?" I asked, unable to keep the disappointment from my voice.

"No laptop," Henry repeated. "Nothing in there except an expired registration and a couple of unpaid parking tickets."

Damn it. And I'd been so certain that Jeffrey Sellers must have stashed the laptop in the trunk or under the seat.

"Oh, well," I said. "It was just a thought. Have a good one, Henry."

And I made myself turn away from him and head toward the guest parking space where I'd left my Renegade. I didn't know how long he stood there and watched me go, because I made sure not to look back until I was buckled in and pulling out of my parking place.

The whole time, though, my thoughts wouldn't stop churning.

No laptop in Jeffrey's office, apartment, or car. Maybe he really didn't have one.

Or maybe he had a secret place for stashing his really important stuff. A storage unit, possibly?

That theory made some sense...except that all the evidence I'd gathered so far seemed to indicate he had next to no spare cash. Would he really have sprung for the fifty or sixty bucks a month that even a very small storage unit would have cost?

I didn't have a clue. Little by little, I'd been gathering information about Jeffrey Sellers, formulating a picture of a man who was barely hanging on by his fingernails and therefore would have done whatever he could to avoid paying even the smallest of obligations, like the unpaid parking tickets Henry had found in Jeffrey's abandoned car. All the same, what I'd put together so far was only a blurry mosaic, not a clear picture.

Besides, if he'd rented a storage unit, wouldn't he have kept some paperwork about it in his filing cabinets at his office? Obviously, he didn't have a problem storing sensitive information there, or he would have stashed all the information regarding his divorce and child support somewhere else.

Once again, all I could really think was "maybe."

For all I knew, my initial impression that Jeffrey Sellers didn't have a computer and conducted all his business on his phone was correct. If that was the case, I knew I'd never get access to that phone, because it must be stowed in an evidence locker at the police station, along with whatever other personal effects he'd had on him when he died. Eventually, his family would have to come and retrieve all that, or possibly they'd have someone local take care of it for them. Through all this, I really hadn't heard anything about his immediate family. Were they estranged?

Considering the way he'd appeared to conduct

his personal life, that theory seemed all too plausible to me.

Right now, I wasn't sure what to do next. Well, except get to the shop and apologize to Melanie for returning so much later than I'd planned. It would be easy enough to manufacture a story about things being backed up at the specialist's office, since she still believed I'd driven to Phoenix for some tests related to my pregnancy, but still.

I let out a sigh. I hadn't pulled that particular card when trying to do a reading on this crime, but right then I felt a lot like the Hanged Man, in limbo while I couldn't find a clear way to move ahead.

About all I could do was hope I'd be able to get myself out of this bind in the next couple of days. Otherwise, Archie and Victoria would have to get married with this terrible shadow hanging over them, not to mention a canceled honeymoon.

Well, sometimes the universe worked in mysterious ways. If we were all very, very lucky, maybe it would step in and save the day.

In the meantime, I'd just have to keep moving forward...even if I had no idea where exactly I was going.

12

A Shot in the Dark

LUCKILY, MELANIE DIDN'T SEEM AT ALL annoyed by having to work most of the day without me there at the shop to help her. "It's fine," she assured me. "We got a shipment from Hay House, but I just left it in the storeroom since I couldn't unpack everything and keep an eye out here at the same time."

The shipment wasn't supposed to be here until Wednesday. Most of the time, I would have been glad to have it arrive a couple of days early, but right now, I felt mostly annoyed about the situation. If I'd known it was coming today, I would have at least warned Melanie that she might have to deal with it.

"Thanks for taking care of that," I told her. "Have you eaten lunch yet?"

"No," she said, and I lifted an eyebrow.

"You know it was okay to close things down while you grabbed something to eat."

"I know," she replied. "And actually, I was about to do just that, but then the UPS driver showed up, and I got kind of distracted."

"Well, go ahead and get something now," I said. "I can keep an eye on things here—and take as long as you need."

She shot me a grateful smile, thanked me, and hurried out. I realized then that I was feeling pretty hungry, too, since of course I had eaten nothing since breakfast.

When Melanie comes back, you can go over to Cloud Coffee yourself, I thought, and quelled the urge to text her so she could pick up something for me as well. She was on a well-deserved lunch break, and didn't need to be fetching and carrying for the boss.

A quick glance around the shop told me everything looked exactly as I'd left it, so it didn't appear as if any hordes of marauding tourists had descended in my absence. To be fair, it wasn't just tourists who could make a mess in the store; the groups of high school girls who came in to buy incense and candles and—when they could afford it—jewelry could cause their own form of havoc.

Luckily, though, while I'd been running late,

I'd still gotten back to the store well before the local high school got out at three o'clock, so Melanie had been spared having to deal with the teenage shoppers all on her own.

Because I honestly didn't have that much to do, I puttered around a little, re-shelving a few books that were out of place, rearranging the crystals on the table where they were displayed and basically making it look as though I was busy without doing much of anything in particular.

My cell phone rang from under the counter where I'd stowed my purse, and I hurried over to pull it out and take a look at the screen.

Calvin.

I immediately put the phone to my ear. "I'm so sorry," I said breathlessly. "I was late coming back, and I totally forgot to call you to let you know how it went."

"That's fine," he replied, his tone dry, almost amused. "Henry Lewis let me know about how he bumped into you at Jeffrey Sellers' apartment."

Oops. "I didn't break in," I said, knowing I sounded way too defensive.

"I know that," Calvin replied. "Henry told me there was no sign of forced entry. Nothing missing, either, unless someone took that laptop we're all looking for."

If it existed at all. "The entire trip wasn't much

use," I confessed. "I mean, it definitely reinforced my belief that Jeffrey Sellers was a world-class jerk, but NancyAnne really didn't tell me anything we didn't already know."

"Well, I don't think it was a total loss," my husband said. "For one thing, Henry seems to be pretty mellow about the situation. I thought he called me just to rat you out, but he actually wanted to let me in on a few additional details about the case."

"He did?" I responded, honestly surprised. While the police chief had clearly given up on trying to dissuade me from conducting my own independent investigations into Globe's murders, I'd never thought he'd be happy about it.

A small chuckle came through my phone's speaker. "Yes, I was just as shocked as you are. But he told me he doesn't believe Victoria is guilty, especially now that he's gotten the preliminary toxicology report. Apparently, what killed Jeffrey Sellers was a dose of atropine."

"'Atropine'?" I repeated. I knew I'd heard the word before, but I had absolutely no idea exactly what it was.

"It's a drug used during anesthesia," Calvin replied. "It's usually administered intravenously, but it can also be swallowed. There were high levels in Jeffrey Sellers' bloodstream and in the creamer the lab tested, so that's why he collapsed so quickly after drinking that coffee. It basically shut down his nervous system."

A chill went through me. Maybe it was a slightly better way to go than the stomach pain and convulsions Aaron Galloway had suffered after drinking a cup of arsenic-laced coffee backstage at his tent revival, but still.

Someone must have really hated Jeffrey Sellers to come up with such a cold-blooded means of ensuring his demise.

"But that's why Henry thinks Victoria couldn't have done it," my husband went on. "Atropine isn't the kind of thing you can exactly pick up at Walgreens or on a street corner somewhere. It's a highly regulated drug that's only stocked in hospitals and other medical facilities that administer general anesthesia."

I nodded...but then another little shiver trickled its way down my spine. "Like the medical center where Sara Tilden works? She's a respiratory therapist."

A long pause. Then Calvin said, "Probably. Do you really think she could have done it?"

There was a question. On the surface, Sara had seemed nothing but friendly and helpful. But what if all that had been nothing more than a front designed to put me off the scent? What if she'd known Jeffrey Sellers was divorced, and had sent us to his office so we could find the incriminating paperwork about his ex-wife and his unpaid child support, and wanted to make it seem as if NancyAnne had much more of a motive for killing him?

I really didn't want to think that about her. Right now, though, I had to consider every possible angle, and that meant adding Sara Tilden back to our list of suspects, especially since I didn't have the auras to rely on, not with my powers being checked by the child in my womb.

A sudden thought occurred to me, and I said, "Calvin, do you know what NancyAnne's occupation is? She never mentioned anything about that to me, but she must work somewhere."

"Hang on a sec," he said. "I'll need to look at that file Ben put together for me."

"Sure."

I waited, phone pressed to my ear, while my husband presumably went searching for the file somewhere in one of the stacks on his perpetually messy desk at the station. The whole time, I could feel the seconds ticking by, and prayed Melanie wouldn't return at this extremely inopportune time. True, there wasn't anything about the situation that I necessarily had to keep from her, but—

Calvin came back, sounding excited. "She's an LVN."

Licensed vocational nurse. A nervous little thrill went through me. Had I let NancyAnne go too easily? Was she now laughing her way back to Iowa, thinking she'd gotten the better of me and the local police?

"Would she have access to atropine?" I asked.

"It depends on where she was working," my husband said. A sound like him ruffling a couple of pages, probably in the file he was holding, and he added, "Looks like she works in a nursing home in Davenport."

Hmm. I had no idea whether a nursing home would stock something like atropine. "Would a place like that have atropine on hand?"

"I doubt it," Calvin said. "I mean, I obviously can't say for sure, but usually those sorts of drugs are used for people going under general anesthesia, and that's not the sort of thing you'd do at an elder-care facility. Any of the residents who needed surgery would be sent to a local hospital for their procedures."

So much for that idea. Or maybe not. Just because NancyAnne wouldn't have access to atropine at the facility where she worked didn't mean she couldn't still have gotten her hands on it somehow. Maybe she was friends with a nurse who worked at a hospital nearby, or someone who was an anesthesiologist at a surgery center. Drugs like that would be locked up, of course, but I knew people stole drugs from hospitals all the time.

Even so, it seemed much more likely that Sara was our real culprit. She worked in an honest-to-Goddess medical center, and probably wouldn't have had too hard a time stealing the drug she needed.

Of course, that made me circle back to exactly why Sara Tilden would have wanted to kill Jeffrey Sellers. She'd claimed they weren't romantically involved, but she could have been lying. How would I have even known whether or not she was telling the truth, now that my auras had deserted me?

I tried to tell myself I shouldn't be overly dramatic. All right, I didn't have those auras to work with right now, but they'd never been one-hundred percent reliable in the first place. Despite everything, I wanted to think my gut instincts about people were still pretty good, and I honestly couldn't see Sara as a cold-blooded killer, no matter how hard I tried.

Yeah, that and four bucks would get me a latte. A feeling about a person certainly wasn't enough to ensure their guilt or innocence.

Well, I'd have to hash that out later…and try to decide whether I should attempt a follow-up interview with Sara, or whether I should take my suspicions to Henry and see what he thought. He'd probably laugh me out of his office, but at least I would have tried.

Speaking of the police chief....

"If Henry Lewis doesn't think Victoria is the killer, why won't he drop the charges against her?" I demanded. "There's no point in having this hanging over hers and Archie's heads if she's not a suspect."

"Probably because it's really in the D.A.'s hands now," Calvin responded. "Also, just because Henry has a feeling about something doesn't mean he plans to change course. It's entirely possible the D.A. will also decide Victoria couldn't be the culprit now that the cause of death has at least a preliminary determination, but that's his call to make, not Henry's. And I know the guy—Alan Crocker likes his conviction rate, and he's not the kind of person who backs down easily."

Which was probably why he'd become a district attorney in the first place, but that particular piece of information didn't make me feel any better about the situation.

Actually, it made me feel a whole lot worse. I didn't want some legal bulldog deciding my friend's fate, not when his judgment might be based on wanting to maintain a sterling track record and not because he'd hadn't actually looked at the facts of the case and judged them on their own merits.

The news did make me feel just a teeny bit better, though. Maybe the D.A. would still insist on sending the case to trial, but I had to believe a jury would look at the evidence and realize Victoria couldn't get her hands on a bunch of atropine any more than she could dig her way into Fort Knox and load up a wheelbarrow with gold bars. She'd still miss out on her honeymoon, but at least she wouldn't be in prison.

I didn't like that scenario, though. Victoria and Archie shouldn't be denied their wedding trip just because someone had done a pretty handy job of framing her.

Before I could say anything else, Melanie returned, and I said hastily, "I'll talk to you more tonight, sweetie. Have a good rest of your day!"

Calvin chuckled. "Did your assistant just come in?"

"Something like that."

"Then here's a kiss to hold you over until tonight." He made a smooching sound into the phone, and we ended the call there.

"Was it busy over at Cloud Coffee?" I asked Melanie. She'd been gone long enough that it looked as though she must have eaten at the coffee shop, or maybe sat in the park to have her sand-

wich, since she was now only carrying her ubiqui-
tous go-cup of iced tea. "I haven't had a chance to
eat yet."

"No, it was pretty quiet, since it's mostly after
lunch," she replied. "But please go eat. I would
have waited for you if I'd known you hadn't
stopped for lunch while you were out."

I smiled at her worried expression and hoped
she wasn't beating herself up for having her own
midday meal before her pregnant boss. "It's okay.
But thanks for covering for me just a little longer."

With that handled, I retrieved my purse from
under the counter and headed out, my pace brisk.
It wasn't just that I was hungry; with the hour
inching past two-thirty, I knew I had a limited
amount of time to get to Cloud Coffee before
they closed at three. Worst-case scenario, I could
always walk a little farther and head over to
Olamendi's for some takeout, but grabbing a
sandwich seemed a lot easier.

As I walked, I couldn't help brooding over the
news Calvin had just given me. Why atropine?
That seemed like a pretty specific drug to give
someone, the kind of compound the killer must
have known could be administered orally and
would act fast, even if it was usually given intravenously. Once again, that pointed to someone
with a background in the healthcare industry,

someone who would have both the knowledge and means to use a toxin that most people wouldn't have even heard of. There were plenty of herbal compounds that could have had the same effect and been much easier to procure.

Come to think of it, you could whip up a pretty decent batch of cyanide if you had the patience to process a bunch of apricot pits to extract the necessary elements.

But even putting aside the poison used and how it had been administered, I kept wondering what exactly Jeffrey Sellers had done to make someone think it was a good idea to poison him. I had enough experience with murders carried out in all sorts of circumstances to know that, contrary to the public's worries about random violence, these sorts of acts tended to be deeply personal. Sometimes, like in poor Danny Ortega's case, it wasn't really murder at all, but a horrible mix-up made by someone who shouldn't have been dabbling in love potions and had brewed him an elixir filled with deadly foxglove rather than ordinary campanula. Still, it wasn't a stranger who'd dipped the fatal love potion into his drink at that Halloween party, but a woman he'd worked with and who harbored an unrequited fascination for the man.

And that told me something else just as personal was at work here, even if I couldn't yet guess what had tipped the murderer over the edge. NancyAnne Nielsen definitely had a motive for wanting Jeffrey dead, but....

But...did she? After all, he'd promised her he was going to pay off her back child support. Why would she kill a man who was going to make a whole lot of her problems go away?

Except for the way it sounded like he lied about pretty much everything? I asked myself. *Maybe she figured out he was just blowing hot air and snapped.*

That didn't feel right, though. A person "snapped" and shot the person who'd wronged them, or maybe pushed them down the stairs in a fit of fury. Securing that atropine and slipping it into the creamer in Victoria's studio fridge seemed to be the actions of someone who was cool and calculating, who could keep their head whether they were stealing drugs from a locked cabinet in a hospital or sneaking in to Victoria's studio to doctor that creamer.

NancyAnne Nielsen had appeared brittle, like a woman teetering on the edge of her breaking point. I honestly couldn't see her doing any of those things...or at least, doing them and not getting caught.

The same for Sara Tilden, although I thought it might still be a good idea to try talking to her once again, if only to satisfy myself that she was no more a cold-blooded killer than I was. It would have to be after work, though, because I'd already taken enough time away from the shop this week.

I could only hope that Calvin would be all right with us taking a return trip to Gilbert….

Because my husband was a mensch of the first order, he didn't argue with my plan, and only asked me if I thought I was stretching myself a little too thin. I assured him I wasn't, and he just said it was fine to go back to Gilbert if I thought it would do any good.

"I'll let you know after I talk to Sara," I told him, and he smiled.

"Good enough for me."

That was why we were headed west at a little after six, with the lowering sun blazing full into our eyes. I'd already texted Sara and asked her if we could talk again, and she'd said it was fine, and that she'd be home by six-thirty.

Meaning we should be done with our chat in plenty of time for Calvin and me to go to our favorite Cajun place in downtown Gilbert, and have a nice dinner that would make up for the drive in case it turned out I didn't learn anything new.

When Sara answered the door, she was still in

her mint-green scrubs, telling me she hadn't had time to get changed after work. Her expression was game, if a bit puzzled, and just like the first time I'd visited, she offered me a seat in the living room and then asked if I'd like a glass of water.

Maybe accepting some water from a woman I wasn't sure was a poisoner wasn't the best idea in the world, but I was thirsty, since Calvin and I had hurried out of the house almost as soon as he got home, and neither of us had stopped to fill our go-cups.

"That would be great, thanks," I told her.

She headed off to the kitchen, where I heard what sounded like her filling a glass from the dispenser in the refrigerator door. That reassured me somewhat, since I figured it would be pretty hard to tamper with something that was coming right out of the appliance, rather than being poured from a pitcher or even from the tap.

Also, she had a glass for each of us when she returned. I took one of them from her and waited for her to take a seat at the opposite end of the sofa. Her gaze was questioning, and I figured there wasn't any point in beating around the bush.

Besides, just like before, I had Calvin waiting for me in the car, and a text message ready to go to ask for help in case I needed it.

"We found out that Jeffrey was poisoned with atropine."

Sara's big blue-gray eyes flared wide…and then almost as quickly sharpened with realization. "That's why you're here? Because you think I had access to the drug?"

"Well, do you?" I asked simply.

A few seconds passed while she appeared to deliberate how much she should tell me. "We have it in the drug locker at work," she said. "But it's strictly monitored."

Since I'd already guessed she would say something along those lines, I didn't let her reply dissuade me. "But could someone get it out of there if they really wanted to?"

"I don't know. Maybe."

She sounded more annoyed than worried, as if she didn't like admitting that the security measures in place at her work weren't quite as good as the people in charge wanted to think they were.

"But I didn't take it," she added, her tone insistent. "Really, do you think I'd be stupid enough to use a drug that I have access to daily at my work?"

Her gaze met mine steadily, challenging me to answer. Was she bluffing?

"No," I said, since there wasn't any other real way to reply. "I don't think you're stupid. But I also think that maybe you aren't telling me the complete story."

Now she blinked and looked away, and I noticed how her fingers tensed around the glass she held before she lifted it to her lips and took a careful sip. However, she didn't seem interested in replying, and appeared much more fascinated by the cheerful bunch of yellow alstroemeria that bloomed on the side table in the tiny foyer.

"Was it something about Jeffrey?" I persisted.

Sara set down the glass. "Okay," she said in a small, tight voice. "Maybe I wasn't totally honest with you before."

"About what?" I asked, knowing how disingenuous that question was.

She must have thought the same thing, because she sent me a withering look. "About there not being anything between the two of us. We were seeing each other when he died."

This admission came out in short, clipped tones, as though she needed to keep as tight a rein on her emotions as possible rather than risk breaking down in front of someone who was next to a stranger.

What was it with that guy? He hadn't been particularly good-looking, and it wasn't as though he was rolling in money or possessed any other redeeming qualities that would have seemed desirable to a single woman.

Maybe he'd been a silver-tongued devil, the kind of man who would promise a woman the moon and have her believe it. As a Gemini myself, I had a deep-seated distrust of anyone who seemed too glib, so I doubted I would have fallen for that act.

But NancyAnne Nielsen had, and Sara Tilden, too…apparently.

"I'm sorry," I said, even if I privately thought Sara could do much better. As my mother often said, however, there was no accounting for taste.

"That's not all, though," she went on, as if now that she'd gotten started, she wanted to unburden herself before she lost her nerve. "I kept getting the feeling he was seeing someone else, although when I confronted him over it, he told me I was imagining things and that he hadn't even looked at another woman after we started dating."

Now it was my turn to lift my glass of water to my lips and take a sip. Bad enough that both NancyAnne and Sara had been taken in by Jeffrey Sellers—and the Goddess only knows how many others in between—but he'd also been dating someone on the side?

Mr. Sellers had been a very busy man.

"What made you think he was seeing someone?" I asked.

"Just little things," Sara said. "He'd break off dates at the last minute, or would tell me he couldn't practice with me because he had a client meeting."

"Well, that doesn't seem too strange," I replied, "considering he was a private detective."

Her lip curled. "Oh, I know he had to keep weird hours sometimes. But after the last time he bailed on me, I got curious, so I drove by his office after work, figuring I'd see his car in the parking lot if he really was meeting a client. When I got there, though, the whole place was empty. He lied."

I had to admit that anecdote did seem a little damning, although I supposed there could have been some logical explanation for why he wasn't there. Maybe his client had wanted to meet at a restaurant or bar, or had canceled their appointment. If that was the case, though, you'd think he would have reached out to Sara to see if he could still see her that evening, despite everything.

"That does sound kind of suspicious," I admitted. "Did you confront him about it?"

"No," Sara replied. I noticed how she didn't quite want to meet my eyes, although I couldn't tell for sure whether it was because she was hiding something or was simply embarrassed to have been forced to admit her romantic connection to Jeffrey Sellers. She went on, "I didn't have any actual evidence, and I guess I convinced myself I was just being paranoid. I'd never had an experience like that before—with the other men I've dated, it was good until it...wasn't. But I never had any reason to believe someone might be cheating on me." She stopped there, an entirely unconvincing smile pulling at her mouth. "I don't suppose you found anything in those file cabinets to prove he was dating someone else at the same time he was seeing me?"

"Nothing like that," I told her, then hesitated. When I'd first found the evidence of Jeffrey Sellers' first marriage in his files, I'd decided not to say anything to Sara about NancyAnne, figuring since Sara hadn't been involved with him, there hadn't been much point in revealing the whole sordid story.

But she *had* been seeing him…which meant she was a better liar than I'd thought, and also that my gut instincts were definitely falling down on the job here.

Oh, what the hell. Who knew…maybe making such a shocking revelation would provoke a reaction that told me Sara really was the murderer, even if she'd almost convinced me with her innocent act.

"Did you know he'd been married in Iowa and had a child there?"

"*What?*"

Well, that outburst seemed to signal that Sara hadn't known about that particular piece of Jeffrey Sellers' checkered past.

"Yes," I said calmly. "We—I," I corrected

myself, since I still hadn't made any mention of how my police chief husband had been providing me with backup in all this, "found his divorce paperwork in his office, along with a whole bunch of unpaid child support claims."

Sara stared at me. She'd set down her glass of water, and now her fingers were taut against the knees of her mint-green scrubs, almost white even though she had a light tan. "That unbelievable bastard," she whispered. "No wonder someone killed him."

The disgust in her voice was pretty damn convincing. True, she'd fooled me before, but some things were a lot harder to fake. And as someone in a profession dedicated to providing care to others, she probably hated the thought of the man she'd been seeing leaving his own child in the lurch like that.

Then a bitter smile tugged at the corner of her mouth, and she said, "Maybe his ex-wife killed him."

"Oh, the thought definitely crossed my mind," I said easily. "But when I talked to her—"

"You—" Sara broke off there and stared at me, consternation obvious in every plane of her face. "You *talked* to her?"

"Yes," I replied. "She was here in Arizona, trying to collect some of that back child support. Jeffrey put her off, telling her he was about to come into a lot of money and that he'd pay her then." I stopped there and fixed Sara with what I hoped was a reasonable facsimile of the steely-eyed stare I'd seen Henry Lewis use on so many occasions. "You wouldn't know anything about that, would you?"

She shook her head. "About him getting an inheritance or something? No, I never heard anything about that."

"I'm not talking about an inheritance," I said, maintaining eye contact so she could tell I was telling the truth. "I'm talking about the money he was trying to extort from Archie Bradshaw and Victoria Parrish."

"Extort?" Sara repeated, and her eyes widened again. "You mean blackmail?"

I nodded.

"But why would Jeffrey want to do that to Archie and Victoria? They're some of the nicest people I've ever met...well, Victoria, anyway," Sara amended quickly, as if she'd seen the way my mouth had quirked at that description of Archie.

This was the part where I couldn't really tell the truth about my friend, the former cat. "I don't know," I said. "Jeffrey must have made them a target because they were prospering and he wasn't. But someone else must have known about his plans, or they wouldn't have known he was going to meet with Victoria last Friday at her studio."

"I don't have any idea who it could have been," Sara said dubiously. "He really didn't have anyone in his life—at least, as far as I could tell."

Except possibly the hypothetical other woman, who might or might not exist.

I also couldn't help noticing how Sara hadn't tried to protest that Jeffrey would never stoop to anything as low as blackmail. She might have had her doubts about why he would have targeted Archie and Victoria, but she clearly believed he was capable of doing such a thing, especially when you considered how dire his financial straits had been.

Which I supposed was interesting from a moral standpoint, but it didn't help me get any closer to finding out who had known about Jeffrey's meeting with Victoria and had taken steps to poison that carton of creamer in her fridge with atropine, thus ensuring he'd never meet with anyone else after that fateful morning.

"Well, someone knew," I said, my tone as tired as I currently felt. Maybe it would be much worse when I was eight or nine months pregnant, but even now I could tell I wasn't nearly as physically ready for this kind of running around as I'd been back before I was carrying another human being inside me. Part of that tiredness was probably just sheer frustration at not being able to get any kind

214 • CHRISTINE POPE

of handle on who had been responsible for Jeffrey Sellers' death, but still.

"I suppose so," Sara responded, sounding nearly as weary as I did. This probably wasn't the sort of thing she'd wanted to wrestle with after working a full day at the medical center. She shifted where she sat, adding, "Was there anything else? I've told you everything I know."

Which wasn't as much as I'd hoped. But even though Sara technically had access to atropine at her work, and even though most people would probably have agreed she had a motive to poison Jeffrey by way of her suspicions about there being another woman involved somehow, I still didn't think she was our murderer.

I couldn't be sure, though. Not without being able to see her aura…not when I was second-guessing myself pretty much every step of the way. She would definitely have to stay in the "maybe" column for now.

"No, there's nothing else," I told her, hoping she couldn't hear the disappointment and worry in my voice, and stood. "Thanks for talking with me again."

A shrug. I noticed how she didn't say it was no problem, probably because it kind of was.

I didn't comment, of course. No, I just headed to the front door and let myself out, gladder than ever that at least I'd have some jambalaya to fortify me before Calvin and I headed home.

Maybe Sara was our murderer and maybe she wasn't, but I knew I'd need a lot more evidence to convince me one way or another than what I currently had in hand.

13

Your Cheating Heart

CALVIN WASN'T QUITE AS DEJECTED AS I WAS, but even he seemed a little subdued during dinner. "Something will come to you," he told me as he handed over a basket of sourdough rolls.

"It hasn't so far," I returned, then selected a roll and put the basket back down on the table.

But sourdough rolls had their way of cheering me up—oh, those luscious carbs—and a few bites made me feel a little better about the world, my mind already working at the problem and trying to see if there was some other way we could approach this.

"If Jeffrey really was seeing someone on the side," I said after swallowing a bite of roll, "would there maybe be credit card transactions or something to show he'd taken her out to dinner or whatever?"

Calvin had just scooped himself a bite of jambalaya, so he had to wait until he was done chewing before he could reply. "It's possible, although he seemed like the kind of person who would have done everything on a cash basis so there wasn't a paper trail."

"Still," I said, and paused. I supposed this kind of digging around wasn't much different from what Ben Ironhorse had done to locate NancyAnne Nielsen's itinerary and let us know she was here in Arizona, but for some reason, it felt much more personal. "Could your deputy take a poke around in Jeffrey Sellers' bank statements to see if he can find anything that looked unusual?"

That request got me the slightest narrowing of my husband's dark eyes. Being Calvin, though, he considered my question carefully before he offered a reply.

"He might," he allowed. "But I'm still not sure if we're going to find anything of interest."

"If you have any other suggestions, I'd love to hear them."

My husband's head tilted, as if he was turning over various possibilities in his mind before discarding them one by one. "We could try interviewing some of his neighbors to see if any of them saw any women coming and going from Jeffrey's apartment. Because we already know what

Sara Tilden looks like, if they report having seen someone who doesn't match her description, then the mystery woman might be the person he was seeing on the side."

I supposed that was possible. On the other hand....

"Do you really think he would have brought someone like that to his apartment?" I asked next. "You'd think he'd want to go to her place so there wouldn't be any chance of his neighbors noticing anything out of the ordinary."

If they were even that observant at all. When I had visited the place, it seemed like the kind of apartment complex where people worked long hours and didn't have much time left over for spying on their neighbors. At least, I hadn't seen a single occupant while we were there. True, it had been in the middle of the day, but in general, you'd usually glimpse at least one person coming and going after taking a late lunch or whatever.

"Well, are you going to do the legwork?" I asked. "I put Melanie off today with a story about getting some tests done in Phoenix, but sooner or later, she's going to wonder why I keep taking off in the middle of the day."

And yes, she probably knew about my amateur sleuthing if she'd talked to anyone in Globe at all, but I still didn't feel like going into a lot of explanations.

"I can do it," Calvin said easily. "Or at least, I'll try. If Hector Salazar's cows decide to start marauding again, I might not have a chance to get away."

I made a face at him, and he grinned, telling me it had mostly been a joke…mostly. The cows could probably wait, but if a genuine emergency came up, Calvin's fact-finding mission at Jeffrey Sellers' apartment complex would have to be put aside until later.

Still, I'd take it, if it meant I could have a relatively quiet day at the shop and not have to go chasing hither and yon. I wanted to do whatever I could to help Victoria out of this mess, but at the same time, I needed to think of my baby's health.

"It's a deal," I told my husband, glad that we had some kind of plan of action.

Even if I wasn't sure whether it would yield any useful information.

One good thing was that I did manage to schedule mani/pedis for Victoria and Hazel and me at a local nail salon late Thursday afternoon, so that was one less thing to worry about. Maybe it would be a subdued celebration because of this mess of a murder case, but at least we'd all have pretty toes at the wedding.

"Thank you for doing that," Victoria said. We were upstairs at her studio in her workroom, where she was surrounded by sketches and swatches and little boards with various tile samples mounted on them. It was just a little after five, and I'd closed up the shop and sent Melanie home. I hadn't heard anything yet from Calvin, who'd texted me to say things were quiet at the station and so he was going to drive out to Mesa to see what he could find, but honestly, I guessed he would wait until we were both back home so we could discuss his findings—if any—over dinner.

"Oh, it was the least I could do," I told her. Because of all my running around, I hadn't had a lot of time to tell either her or Archie what I'd found out so far, which admittedly wasn't much. However, letting Victoria know that at least our manicures weren't at risk gave me the opportunity to also fill her in on the little we'd discovered about Jeffrey Sellers' past, as well as our possible subjects. "I'm still not sure whether it was even Sara Tilden or NancyAnne Nielsen, though," I concluded. "Calvin's trying to find out about the mystery woman, the one Jeffrey was supposedly seeing. Maybe she's our real culprit."

"Does Henry Lewis know about any of this?" Victoria asked. She'd listened to my recitation with the faintest of lines between her perfectly arched brows, telling me she was probably more disturbed by all of it than she wanted to let on.

"Some," I said. "Not everything. If I'd picked up even the slightest hint that one of those women might have been the person who spiked your creamer with atropine, then I would have passed along the information to him. As it is, I didn't really see the point."

"I guess not," she replied, and released the faintest of sighs. "It's all so frustrating."

"It is," I agreed. I reached for the glass of water she'd poured for me, took a sip, and then gave it a speculative glance as a sudden thought struck me.

Victoria must have noticed where I was looking, because she said, "What?"

"The creamer," I said slowly. "You never use it, right?"

"No," she replied at once. "I don't even drink coffee. Just plain black tea for me, either hot or iced. I keep the coffee and creamer here for my clients."

"Which means the killer must have known there wasn't a chance you would have drunk the poison," I told her. "Otherwise, it was a pretty risky method of murdering someone, since there would always be the chance that you'd use the creamer yourself before you even had a chance of pouring it into a guest's coffee."

She blinked. "I hadn't thought of that."

Neither had I...until right now. What it meant, exactly, I didn't know for sure, except that it seemed clear the murderer had targeted Jeffrey specifically, using a method that would leave Victoria unscathed.

Physically, anyway. She was still in a lot of legal trouble.

But what about Victoria's clients? True, it wasn't as though she had people coming and going from her studio all the time, and now that she was occupied with the model homes for the Mariposa Heights development, she was focused on that. It sure seemed to me like the killer must have been aware of that, and therefore had been confident that no one except Jeffrey Sellers would be at the studio...and therefore be the beneficiary of Victoria's hospitality.

That idea disturbed me more than anything else. It meant that whoever it was, they were familiar enough with my friend's schedule and her client roster that there hadn't been too much danger of anyone else consuming that atropine-laced creamer.

Someone on the Mariposa Heights team? They knew all about Victoria's comings and goings, although again, I couldn't think of a single reason why anyone who worked for the company would want to kill Jeffrey Sellers.

Unless one of his private investigations had

destroyed that person's marriage? After all, he'd boasted to Sara Tilden about doing that very thing.

"What's wrong?" Victoria asked, clearly noticing the shift in my expression.

"I'm not sure," I said. Because all I had was an underlying sense of unease, I really didn't want to upset her by commenting that I thought the murderer must have been paying a lot of attention to her comings and goings...or to make her suspect that one of the very people who'd hired her might have had something to do with Jeffrey Sellers' death. "I guess I'm just trying to put all the pieces together and not getting very far."

Even though it was her freedom on the line if this all went horribly sideways, Victoria was still quick to defend my efforts. "I think you've collected a lot of information in a very short period. You shouldn't beat yourself up because this isn't going as fast as you want it to."

I managed a wan smile. "Are you forgetting that if I don't get this figured out in the next couple of days, you aren't going on your honeymoon?"

"No, I hadn't forgotten," she responded at once, giving me a smile that was much more cheerful than the one I'd sent her way only a moment earlier. "But I'm just going to keep hoping. Archie and I haven't canceled our reservations because we were already past the point where we could have gotten our deposits back. So even if you don't identify the murderer until the moment when Archie and I are saying, 'I do,' it'll still be fine."

I definitely had to admire her optimism. Somehow, I doubted I would be feeling the same way if our situations had been reversed.

But I got the message. Victoria planned to keep sailing ahead no matter what happened, and I knew I needed to take my cues from her.

Before I could reply, the studio door opened, and Archie came in. I hadn't seen him for a couple of days, and although he looked a little more strained than his fiancée, I could tell he was trying to keep his chin up for her sake.

"I hope I'm not interrupting—" he began, and Victoria shook her head.

"No, Selena's just catching me up on a few bits and pieces," she told him. "And I was about to start getting my things together when she got here, so I'll be ready to go soon."

She sent me a questioning glance then, as if asking whether I had anything else to add.

It had been on the tip of my tongue to mention that Chief Lewis really didn't believe in her guilt, but I decided to keep quiet for now. If it had been just the two of us, she might have accepted that piece of information and carefully tucked it away, but I knew if Archie had heard that kind of declaration, he would have marched right over to the police station and told Henry he needed to do whatever he could to get the charges dropped.

True, Henry probably wasn't even there, since it was now well past five and, unlike Calvin, he kept a pretty regular eight-to-five schedule. Clearly, he thought his rank afforded him that privilege.

But since I doubted Archie would have let the matter go so easily, I had to believe he would have been right in Henry's face first thing the next morning.

"No, that's pretty much it," I said. "If I think of anything else, I'll let you know." My gaze strayed to the stacks of sample books and notes on the table, which Victoria had already started gathering up. "I thought you weren't going to work past Wednesday."

"I'm not," she replied. "That's part of the reason why I wanted to take some of this stuff home, just in case."

"By which she means she can pretend to be taking the time off, but actually be working at the house," Archie observed dryly. "But that's all right —I plan to hide it all so she can't focus on anything except the wedding."

She lifted an eyebrow, but since her mouth

curved in amusement at the same time, I got the feeling she knew he was joking.

Mostly.

And I could understand why she'd want to distract herself with her work. The wedding wasn't going to be some huge, over-the-top sort of event, but a quiet ceremony in their backyard, with a small reception to follow. She was only expecting twenty-five guests, and I guessed she could probably have put together that sort of event in her sleep and with her hands tied behind her back.

I rose from my seat and said, "Well, I'll get out of your hair. If I don't see you before then, I'll meet you at five-thirty on Thursday at Paradise Nails."

"Absolutely," she replied.

As I left, I couldn't help wondering about those uncanceled reservations for their honeymoon. I'd believed Victoria when she'd said it was too late to get their deposits back, but if they were no-shows at the last minute, wouldn't they lose the entire cost of their lodgings?

I supposed it depended on the policies of the various places they were staying. All the same, I couldn't wait to get home and hear what—if anything—Calvin had discovered during his stakeout at Jeffrey Sellers' apartment.

More than I'd expected, actually. Because I'd started a batch of chicken cacciatore in the crock pot before I left that morning, there wasn't much to do to prepare the meal except boil the spaghetti and throw a salad together. Calvin had already texted me to say he was on his way home and would be there a little before seven, so I was just setting down the big bowl of pasta when the front door opened.

He kissed me on the cheek, said, "That smells amazing," and then headed into the powder room so he could get washed up before our meal.

But then we were both sitting down at the table, and I sent him an expectant look. "Well?"

"Well, I learned a couple of things," Calvin replied, and waited for me to hand him the bowl of tossed green salad.

"Such as?"

He helped himself to some romaine and tomatoes, and said, "Jeffrey Sellers definitely sounds like he was a player. The woman who rents the apartment next to his is really young, a student at ASU. She told me she and her roommate were both hit on by him several times, even though they made it as obvious as possible that they weren't interested."

Definitely not. He had to have been at least thirteen or fourteen years older than they were. I decided that saying "ew" wouldn't be very mature, so I settled for asking, "Anything else?"

Calvin's mouth quirked, and he took a bite of salad before replying. "Kaitlyn—the girl I talked to—said she thought Sellers had two different women coming and going from his place. Her description of one of them definitely sounds like it was Sara Tilden, but she said the second woman had blonde hair and looked like she was maybe in her early thirties. Problem is, Kaitlyn never got a very good look at her, so she couldn't give me much more of a description than that."

I ate a grape tomato, pondering this latest development. It was too bad that Jeffrey's next-door neighbor hadn't been able to notice much beyond the second woman having blonde hair, but at least that told me we were talking about two different people here, since Sara Tilden's hair was obviously brown.

Then again, NancyAnne Nielsen had blonde hair, although it was the dark dishwater kind that some people might have described as light brown.

"How blonde was the woman?" I asked.

Calvin had been right in the middle of slurping up a piece of spaghetti, so I had to wait until he was done before he could reply. "Kaitlyn said she had very light blonde hair, almost platinum. So…sounds like pretty blonde to me."

Then that definitely wasn't NancyAnne.

Which meant the person Jeffrey's neighbor had seen must have been the "other" woman.

Unless she was an acquaintance, or a client, or someone else from the ballroom dance community. Just because Jeffrey Sellers seemed as though he was always on the prowl didn't mean there might not have been a perfectly innocent explanation why the blonde woman had been spotted at his apartment.

Yeah, right.

"Jeffrey's neighbor didn't notice anything else about her?" I asked, knowing I sounded way too desperate. "Height? Build? Clothes?"

My husband's expression was sympathetic, which I supposed counted for something. "I asked about that, but Katelyn just said the woman seemed kind of average—not too tall or too short, not especially thin or heavy. She did say she was wearing jeans and a black top, but that's not exactly the kind of outfit that would stand out."

No, not when it seemed to be the uniform of half the women in Arizona. You'd think they'd choose lighter colors because of the heat and sometimes oppressive sun, but that didn't seem to be the case.

"Well, at least we know it probably wasn't either Sara or NancyAnne," I said, trying not to sound too dejected, and popped a bite of chicken cacciatore into my mouth.

"Doesn't seem that way," Calvin agreed before adding, "I know it doesn't feel like a lot right now, but what Katelyn told me seems to confirm Sara Tilden's claim that Jeffrey was seeing someone else. Now all we have to do is figure out who this woman might be."

"Oh, is that all?" I quipped and reached for my glass of water. More than ever, I wished it was a glass of wine, but I knew that wasn't going to happen. I'd already told myself I could have half a glass of champagne at Archie and Victoria's reception, and that was it for my alcohol consumption this month…and the next five.

"Hey, at least we know she's blonde," my husband told me. "That's more than we knew before today."

He had a point there. And while Arizona some days seemed absolutely packed with blondes ranging from dark dishwater to bright platinum, I knew they were still outnumbered by those of us with dark hair.

The two of us ate in silence for a moment. Then I said, "Do you think it's worth going back to Jeffrey's office and poking around in his files again? I think I could get Sara to loan me the key."

Calvin tapped a finger against the side of his water glass. Like me, he wore the expression of someone who would have been a lot happier if it had contained a nice pinot grigio instead of some San Pellegrino. "We didn't find much the first time," he pointed out.

"We learned about NancyAnne," I replied. "And at the time, we didn't have any reason to be looking for something specifically regarding a woman Jeffrey Sellers might have been seeing. Now we can narrow our search."

A shrug, and Calvin said, "I guess we can give it a try. Do you think you'll be able to take a few hours off tomorrow afternoon?"

"Probably," I said. "It would be better than Thursday, since I'm meeting Hazel and Victoria at the nail salon after work, and I don't want to do anything that might make me late. Then on Friday…."

I let the words trail off, but I knew he understood what I was talking about. On Friday, I was supposed to be over at Archie and Victoria's place, helping to direct traffic as the party-supply people and the florists and the caterers dropped off various bits and pieces. The actual food and flowers wouldn't be delivered until Saturday morning, but still, there were plenty of other things that needed to be managed.

"Well, let's try for tomorrow," Calvin told me. "I'm pretty sure I can slip out for a few hours. After dinner, why don't you text Sara and see if it's okay to pick up the key from her at work?"

That sounded like a plan, so I made a sound of agreement and then returned to my dinner. We kept the conversation pretty low-key after that, both of us seeming to understand there wasn't much point discussing our investigation any further until we knew whether we would have the opportunity to dig through those files again.

But after I sent Sara a message, her reply was disappointing, to say the least.

I wish I could, but your police chief must have figured out that I had a key to Jeffrey's office, b/c he sent a deputy over to confiscate it. I asked them who was going to feed the fish, & they took me to the office so we could bring the tank back to my place. Now I have it sitting in my living room while I try to find someone who can take it permanently...the guy I'd hoped would take it couldn't after all, b/c he's in the middle of moving.

Texts generally weren't very good at conveying a person's emotions, but it didn't take a mind reader to figure out that Sara was pretty annoyed by the whole thing.

Not that I could blame her. That fish tank must have been at least three feet long, and her living room wasn't all that big.

And damn Henry for sticking his nose in it. If he'd waited just another day to confiscate that key, Calvin and I could have gone and poked around, no harm, no foul. As it was, now we'd have to try some other way of figuring out exactly who the mystery blonde could be.

Okay, I knew that was being a bit irrational about the situation, since Henry was only doing his job, but I didn't feel like being rational right then. After all, if a pregnant woman couldn't be illogical from time to time, then who could?

I texted Sara back and said it wasn't a problem, and told her I hoped she would find a home for Jeffrey's fish soon. Then I put down the phone and let out a sigh.

"She won't let you have the key?" Calvin asked from his spot in his favorite chair. We'd come into the living room to settle down after dinner, and he'd turned on the TV but kept it muted so it wouldn't disturb me.

"Henry took it," I said shortly, and released another annoyed breath.

"I guess that's not too surprising," Calvin replied. "I probably would have done the same thing."

Having my husband agree with Henry's actions wasn't the sort of thing that helped my state of mind any. I made a noncommittal sound, and Calvin, correctly gauging my mood, didn't offer any further comments on the subject, but instead turned the sound back on the TV.

Fair enough. I was ready to lose myself in someone else's lives for a while…even as I prayed some other way of identifying the blonde woman would suggest itself to me. We were all doing our best to play it cool, but I couldn't help feeling that time was running out as we sat there watching *Yellowstone.*

Unfortunately, not even a hedgewitch could slow the inexorable passage of time.

14

For Non-Blondes

WHEN I WOKE UP THE NEXT MORNING, however, I wasn't feeling quite as dejected as I had during dinner. That might have been because the sun was shining and I'd slept like a rock the entire night before, but it also could have been because I realized I wasn't quite as without resources as I wanted to believe. I'd consult the Tarot, possibly my pendulum, and, if all else failed, roust my Grandma Ellen from playing canasta in the after-life so she could offer her own input on the situation, even though she'd made it clear on previous occasions that she didn't want me bothering her over every little thing.

Despite that minor complication, I was smiling when I kissed Calvin before he headed off to work a little before eight, and why I hummed to myself as I tidied the kitchen following breakfast, then went into my office, determined to get some answers.

Even if I didn't know for sure what they might be.

Sadie watched me from her bed as I lit some copal incense, hoping the purifying nature of that particular scent would help to clear my mind. For some magical workings, I liked to keep the drapes closed, but this morning, I opened them wide so the clear light of morning could blow away the cobwebs in the corners of my brain and allow me to focus all my intent on discovering exactly who had put that atropine in Victoria's creamer.

As always, I reached for my Tarot deck first, mostly because it was the one tool that gave me the most definitive answers. Rather than waiting for that little tingle to tell me I'd gotten to the right card—since I knew it probably wouldn't happen, not with the way I'd been so blocked over the past few months—I instead shuffled them for a full minute, then deliberately cut them seven separate times. I hoped that using that magically charged number would give this reading a little extra oomph, even if I was sort of flying blind here.

The first card was the Queen of Cups, reversed. The general meaning of that card was emotional immaturity, but I couldn't help noticing the hair color of the woman in the illustration, which was bright blonde.

A tip of the hat toward the unknown blonde woman who'd been spotted coming and going from Jeffrey Sellers' apartment?

Maybe.

Frowning, I drew the second card. There was Old Faithful, aka the Ten of Swords, the card of ultimate betrayal.

So, were the cards telling me Jeffrey Sellers had been murdered by an emotionally immature woman with blonde hair?

Considering that the third and final card I pulled was the Lovers reversed, the answer to that question appeared to be a big old yes.

Problem was, I still had no clue who the blonde woman was, and while this card pull reinforced my belief that she was the one who'd killed Jeffrey, it wasn't helping much when it came to giving me any clues as to her actual identity.

Time to try again.

I picked up the cards and put them back in the deck, then shuffled them for another full minute and cut them the ritual seven times, since that seemed to have worked fairly well on my first attempt.

The first card was the Two of Cups, followed by the Seven of Wands and the Page of Pentacles. No matter how I tried to look at it, this particular combination of cards made little sense, especially when I tried to apply it to my current situation.

Well, you couldn't win 'em all.

Two more follow-up attempts resulted in more of what I called "minor arcana mishmash," so I tucked the cards back into the deck and slid it into the green velvet pouch that kept them safe when I wasn't using them.

Clearly, I needed to try something else, because my success with that first card pull didn't look as though it wanted to repeat itself.

I went over to the bookshelf that held my pendulums and my scrying mats, and chose my favorite, the round one with a beautiful illustration of a luna moth emblazoned on it. In the past, I'd had slightly more luck with my fluorite pendulum than any of the others, so I picked up that one and took it and the mat back over to my altar.

The key problem with pendulums was that it was hard to get anything out of them beyond simple "yes" and "no" answers. Every time I'd tried to have it spell out a name, the pendulum had swung back and forth without settling on any particular letters, telling me that, while some people might have had the talent for coaxing those sorts of answers from their pendulums, I wasn't one of those lucky few.

Instead, I tried to fix what I hoped would be a helpful question in my mind.

Is Jeffrey Sellers' killer the blonde woman who was seen at his apartment?

I held myself as still as possible, knowing that my own movements could jeopardize the reading if I wasn't careful. No, this reply needed to come from the universe and nowhere else.

The pendulum swung back and forth, slowly and deliberately. Hardly daring to breathe, I waited until it had come to a complete stop.

Yes.

I released my breath. True, it was something I'd already suspected, but having the fact confirmed this way told me I was definitely on the right path.

Problem was, I didn't know where that particular path was supposed to lead from here. Without knowing the identity of the woman, I was going to have a hard time bringing her to justice.

But all was not lost. I could still do my best to narrow down where we might find her.

Does the woman live in Mesa?

Again, the pendulum swung back and forth, but there was something uncertain about its movements, as if it wasn't sure where it wanted to land. I waited, knowing I couldn't do anything until it came to a stop.

Which it did…in between "yes" and "no."

I frowned. How could you live in a place and not live there at the same time?

That seemed to be what the pendulum was trying to tell me, although I couldn't quite figure out what that answer was supposed to mean.

Time to move on.

Will she kill again?

The arc of the pendulum seemed even more hesitant this time, and once more stopped in between "yes" and "no."

Meaning…what? That she wasn't planning any other murders at the moment, but she might decide to bust out the atropine again if the situation warranted it?

That particular scenario didn't seem very reassuring.

One more try.

Will I be able to find her?

The pendulum trembled once and was still. Apparently, it wasn't too sanguine about my prospects…and at the moment, neither was I.

Knowing that I probably wasn't going to get any more coherent answers out of the little fluorite drop, I took it and the scrying mat over to my bookshelf and returned them to their designated places. My gaze fell on the crystal ball that sat two shelves down, and I hesitated.

Should I?

Well, I hadn't bothered Grandma Ellen for months. I had to hope she wouldn't be too annoyed by me barging in on her afterlife with some questions.

I took the crystal ball over to my altar, carefully dusted it off—I hadn't had much time lately to keep up with housekeeping in my office—and then said, quietly but urgently, "Grandma Ellen, I need you."

The crystal ball remained quiescent, but I told myself I needed to be patient. Sometimes she appeared right away, and sometimes it took her a few minutes to respond to my call, as though she was off somewhere doing something much more important, and had to find a good stopping place before she appeared inside the crystal.

And sometimes…sometimes she didn't show up at all.

As the seconds ticked by and the crystal ball remained stubbornly clear, I worried that this would be one of those times. Eventually, though, a pale, swirling mist formed inside the crystal, and then I saw my grandmother's face looking back at me.

She'd been in her early forties when she died from uterine cancer, so the woman I saw now appeared to be in the prime of life, pretty and blonde like my mother, with the same blue-gray eyes we all shared. When she spoke, she sounded amused rather than alarmed.

"It's been a while," she said. "How are you and the baby doing?"

"Just fine," I replied. "I feel like I'm getting bigger every day. He or she must take after Calvin."

Although I hoped my baby wouldn't take after him *too* much. My husband had weighed ten pounds when he was born, and I wasn't much looking forward to giving birth to a bowling ball.

"That's good," my grandmother said. Then her head tilted—well, as much as it could within the confines of the crystal ball—and she added, "I suppose this is about that mess with your friend Victoria."

I didn't bother to ask how Grandma Ellen knew about the current situation. While those who'd passed weren't omniscient, they still saw a lot more than we mere mortals did…which was the whole reason why I always came to her for help when the regular forms of divination didn't seem to be helping me very much.

"It is," I said. "I've pretty much figured out that the killer is a blonde woman, but I can't seem to get past that to find out who she actually is. I was hoping you could give me a few clues."

My grandmother lifted a perfectly arched brow. She always wore makeup, or at least appeared to me that way, with soft brown shadow on her lids and her favorite Cherries in the Snow lipstick on a full mouth whose shape had been passed down to both my mother and me. "You know I can't come right out and tell you that."

I'd been halfway expecting an answer along those lines, even as I had to wonder who was calling the shots in the afterlife, telling the spirits of those who'd passed what they could and couldn't say to the living. However, I had a feeling if I tried to ask her about that, she'd just shut me down.

Better to stick to the problem at hand.

"No, but you can give me a couple of hints, can't you?"

Her mouth pursed. "It's not my place to say very much," she responded. "But I can tell you one thing—the answer to your question isn't as far away as you might think."

"It is?" I said, startled. "What…are you saying that the murderer is somewhere nearby? Are they here in Globe?"

"I've told you what I can," Grandma Ellen said. "It's up to you to make that final leap. Good luck, Selena."

She faded away then, and I knew there was no point in trying to call her back. Once she'd spoken, that was it.

No, I'd have to figure it out on my own...to make that "final leap," as she'd said.

I couldn't help thinking that, with my complete lack of helpful information, it would be a leap into the dark.

But I couldn't waste any time brooding over my grandmother's pronouncements, since I needed to head into work. It was important that I be there the whole day —tomorrow was Friday, and I'd already told Melanie I wouldn't be at the shop because I'd be helping Victoria with her wedding prep. My assistant had assured me that wouldn't be a problem, and yet I still didn't think it would be a good idea to ditch her while I went off on some wild goose chase.

Not that there seemed to be any geese worth chasing when it came to this particular mystery. The whole drive in to work, I kept wracking my brains, trying to think of all the blonde women I'd seen in Globe lately, and not coming up with anyone who wasn't a resident and who hadn't been part of the landscape there for years. None of them fit that odd description the pendulum had given me, of someone who both lived here and didn't.

Unless my crazy idea about someone who was

working on the Mariposa Heights development being the actual killer actually had some merit. I thought I'd heard Victoria mention once that the lead architect and a couple of the assistants were renting houses and apartments here in Globe because they didn't want to tackle the long commute from Phoenix.

Was that what Grandma Ellen had meant? It felt like an awfully long shot to me.

Once again, I had that sensation of hitting a brick wall…and I didn't like it one bit.

But being in the shop always made me feel calmer, more centered, and I had to admit it was nice to be there alone for a little while before Melanie showed up. I breathed in the cool, faintly incense-scented air, and stood quietly in the middle of the space for a moment, head tilted up so I could gaze at the beautiful night-sky mural Hazel had painted on the ceiling only a few years ago.

Almost two and a half years now, although it felt as though I'd lived a lifetime in that brief span. I had friends and a life here that I'd never even dreamed of having back when I lived in Los Angeles…and right now, one of those friends needed me.

"Is something wrong with the ceiling?" Melanie asked, and I startled.

"No, no," I said quickly, a little embarrassed

that I'd been so lost in my reverie, I hadn't even heard her approach. "Just letting my mind wander."

She smiled, although there was almost something indulgent in that smile, as if she was thinking I already had a severe case of pregnancy brain even though I was only four months along.

"We're supposed to get a pretty big shipment from Llewellyn Press today," I went on, keeping my tone brisk and businesslike. "When it arrives, you can handle unpacking it while I keep an eye on things up here."

"Sure," she said easily. "I like working in the stockroom."

And thank the Goddess for that, because even now I could tell it wasn't as easy to be bending and lifting as it had been a couple of months ago.

"For now, though," I told her, "you can open things up. Here's the key."

And I handed her a key to the front door, something I'd finally had a chance to get duplicated yesterday while on my lunch break.

"Oh, thanks," she said. "I was wondering how we were going to handle me running the store without you for the next couple of days."

"I'm sorry it took me so long to get around to it," I replied. "But yes, this key works on both the front door and the one in the back. Victoria and I decided that we'll leave the lobby unlocked, since her studio and my store will be locked up, anyway. And I'll show you how to set the alarm when we leave today."

"Sounds good," Melanie said, and hurried off to unlock the front door, since by then it was actually a couple of minutes after ten.

Not that it mattered, since it wasn't as though we had anyone clamoring to get inside that particular Thursday morning.

As the day wore on, though, things got busier, and I was kept on my toes, especially when the promised Llewellyn Press shipment arrived a little after two, and Melanie had to go back to the stockroom to get it unpacked and all the various items put on their designated shelves.

I'd just finished packing up some crystals for a couple of tourists passing through on their way to Payson when Henry Lewis entered the shop. My expression must have been one of utter surprise, because he sent me an ironic smile as he approached the counter.

"Afternoon," he said.

"Hi, Henry," I replied, hoping I sounded at least partly unruffled. "Looking for something for Joyce?"

Maybe one eyebrow lifted ever so slightly. "No," he said. "Our anniversary isn't until next month. I just wanted to come by and let you know I talked to the D.A."

That revelation made me perk up at once, as I was sure he'd intended it to. Still, I tried to be casual as I responded, "And?"

"No soap," he said, and I deflated at once. "He said he'd take my judgment into consideration, but that there was still enough evidence for him to proceed with the case. He's expecting to have a trial date set next week sometime."

Damn it. I supposed I should have been glad that Henry had spoken up at all—he definitely hadn't been required to stick his neck out like that —but still, it didn't appear the D.A. was going to unbend even the slightest inch.

"Well, thank you for asking," I said. I hesitated then, wondering if I should even mention it, but since Henry had shown he was willing to go to bat for Victoria, I figured I might as well make the attempt. "Do you think there's any way to get the judge to loosen up the terms of her bail even the littlest bit? It's going to be awful for Archie and Victoria to lose out on their Napa honeymoon, but if you put in a good word for them, maybe he could have them only stay in the state instead of being stuck here in Globe. At least that way they'd be able to go to Sedona or Flagstaff, or maybe just to the wine country nearby in Willcox and Sonoita."

For one long, uncomfortable moment, Henry just gazed back at me, expression impassive as usual. I was sure he was going to shoot me down, but then he said, "I'll look into it. Don't get your hopes up, though."

"I won't," I replied. "I mean, I won't say anything to Archie or Victoria until you get back to me."

"I'll see what the judge has to say," Henry told me.

He seemed to decide that was the only end cap our conversation required, because he turned away and headed back outside. I lingered behind the counter, sending every positive thought and silent prayer I knew winging out into the universe so my friends would be granted just this smallest bit of grace.

I supposed I'd find out soon enough whether it would be sufficient.

15

Getting Nailed

APPARENTLY, THE UNIVERSE WASN'T LISTENING to my pleas, because Henry called my cell phone about an hour later and said without preamble, "No go. The judge doesn't want your friend leaving town. She and her new husband will just have to amuse themselves here in Globe."

Disappointment shot through me, but I kept my voice level as I said, "Well, thanks for trying, Henry. I appreciate it."

"It was no trouble." A pause, and he went on, "You mean you're not going to swoop in and save the day this time? I was sure you would've nailed our killer by now."

His voice was its usual deadpan self, so it was hard for me to tell if he was joking, especially since I couldn't see his expression. I took his remark at face value and said, "It's not for lack of trying. And if you have any additional pieces of information you'd like to give me, now would be the time."

He chuckled. "I think we're just about as stymied as you are. But if we come up with something, I'll let you know."

After delivering that promise…which I wasn't sure was sincere…he ended the call. I stowed my phone in my purse just as a couple of high school girls came in and headed straight to the incense display. Luckily, they weren't paying any attention to me, because the Goddess only knows what my face must have looked like right then.

The only good thing—if you could even call it that—about this whole mess was that I hadn't said anything to either Archie or Victoria about trying to get the judge to alter the terms of Victoria's bail, so at least I hadn't gotten their hopes up over nothing.

I'd definitely have to do my best to swallow my disappointment, though, or she'd be sure to ask me if something was wrong when I met her and Hazel at Paradise Nails only a few hours from now. She'd probably understand why the judge was being such a jerk, but I preferred for her to stay blissfully ignorant of the whole situation.

Maybe it was for the best. At this late date, I didn't know whether I would have even been able to find a hotel room for Victoria and Archie, no matter how much cash I threw at the problem. Because that had been my plan—to get the judge to alter the terms of her bail, and then surprise the couple by telling them I'd already booked their room and that all they had to do now was go forth and enjoy themselves.

I reminded myself that the important thing was for my friends to have their wedding and enjoy their day. A honeymoon was certainly the cherry on the top of that particular cake, but they could always take their trip later on after we were past all this mess.

Then again, how much could they even relax and allow themselves to have fun at their wedding, knowing that Victoria would be going to trial for a murder she didn't commit? I had no doubt they'd put on brave faces, but there would be a shadow over their special day, no matter how cheerful they might be acting.

Unless, of course, I managed to figure this out before then, and since I didn't have any new clues and it didn't sound as though Henry did, either, I kind of doubted that was going to happen.

Melanie came out from the storeroom then, dusting her hands on the legs of her jeans. "All set," she said cheerfully. "Anything else you need me to do?"

"No, that was it," I replied. "You might as well

take it easy today, since you're going to be working solo tomorrow and Saturday."

That prospect didn't seem to faze her too much, because she only shrugged and said, "I'm sure it'll be fine. But I was wondering if you planned to put up any Halloween decorations? The other stores I've gone into lately seem to have everything set out already."

Getting ready for Halloween had been just about the last thing on my mind the past couple of days, but Melanie was right. If I didn't get my rear in gear, there wouldn't be any point in decorating at all.

"I was," I said, and sighed. "It's just sort of slipped my mind. But we should probably start putting up the decorations. They're in the very back of the stockroom, in a couple of big plastic bins labeled 'Halloween.'"

"Let me handle it," she said. "You can keep an eye on the customers while I work. That way, you won't be over-exerting yourself or anything."

Once again, I found myself surprised by her thoughtfulness. The last couple of years, I'd had to maneuver putting up holiday decorations around helping clients, and I had to admit it could get a little tiring.

"Are you sure?" I asked. The last thing I wanted was to take advantage of her. "It's kind of a big project."

In response, she just sent me a wide smile. "Then I suppose I'd better get started."

She headed back to the stockroom, and a minute later, wheeled out one of the big bins I'd gotten at the Container Store, followed by the second. After that, she started pulling out the various decorations, separating them by type so it would be easier for her to find what she needed once she really got going.

And honestly, I thought she might have been even faster than I was about setting out the haunted trees with their purple lights and the fake gravestones and all the other little bits and pieces that transformed Once in a Blue Moon into a spooky cemetery. Once or twice, she paused so she could ask me a question about the placement of a particular item, but after about an hour, she'd finished the job and was wheeling the now-empty bins back into the stockroom.

"That was amazing," I told her when she came back out. "Were you a professional set designer once upon a time or something like that?"

She gave an amused chuckle. "No, but I took some theater classes in college and worked on the sets for a couple of productions, so I guess this kind of thing just comes naturally to me. But I'm glad you like it."

"I love it," I replied. "And I'm sure my customers will love it, too."

That turned out to be nothing more than the truth, because the people who came into the shop those last couple of hours before closing all praised the decorations, and said they were glad my store was finally getting in the spirit of the season. I was glad, too, because I had a feeling that if I'd delayed putting up my Halloween decorations any longer, I would've had to hand in my witch card.

The day wound down to its end, and at five, Melanie headed over to lock the front door with the key I'd given her. I got my purse out from under the counter and said, "I need to get going, but if anything comes up tomorrow that you're not sure about, just call me. I'll only be a few minutes away at Archie and Victoria's house, and I can come over and help out if you need me to."

"It's going to be fine," Melanie said, almost sternly. "You go help your friends, and don't worry about me. It's not like you're leaving me alone on Black Friday or something."

No, I wasn't, and even at its busiest, I doubted my shop was something my assistant couldn't handle. "All right," I said. "Still, if there's an emergency—"

"There won't be an emergency," Melanie cut in, almost laughing. "It's going to be fine. Now shoo—I'll finish locking up."

Deep down, I knew she was right. The worst that would happen was that a tour bus might disgorge its passengers right in front of the store and she'd be busy for a half hour or so, but that was the most nightmarish scenario I could conjure up.

So I thanked her again for handling everything, and headed out back so I could climb into my Renegade and drive over to Paradise Nails, which was about five minutes away, not too far from the Super Walmart. Hazel was just locking up her ancient but beloved Volvo station wagon as I entered the parking lot, so I pulled into the space next to hers. Victoria's red Mercedes SUV was nowhere to be seen, however.

Well, Hazel and I were both a couple of minutes early, something that surprised me a little. In general, my artist friend wasn't known for her punctuality.

"Hi," I said as I walked over to her car. "Have you heard from Victoria?"

"She sent me a text a few minutes ago that she was running a little late but would be here as soon as she could," Hazel replied. "Something about getting some sketches off to the builder."

That sounded exactly like Victoria. She always put her clients first.

"Well, we might as well go in," I said. "Then she can just join us when she gets here."

Hazel was agreeable with that plan, so we headed inside. Jackie, the Vietnamese woman who owned the salon, obviously had been expecting us, because she guided Hazel and me to a pair of pedicure stations toward the back, and surprised us by offering some chardonnay.

"None for me, thank you," I said, and put a hand on my belly, already more rounded than it had been even a week ago.

Jackie smiled. "Of course, Selena. Some sparkling water, then?"

I said that sounded wonderful, and soon enough, Hazel and I were sitting with our feet in warm water, me with a glass of Perrier in one hand, and Hazel with some chardonnay. We'd just taken our first sips when Victoria hurried in.

"I'm so sorry," she said as she came over. "I was just trying to get all those last little bits done before the weekend got here."

"It's fine," I replied, and paused as Jackie came up and offered Victoria a glass of chardonnay, then pointed at the pedicure station next to mine so she could get situated. "I'm just glad you could make it."

"Oh, Archie would've let me have it if I skipped my spa experience," she said with a laugh. "He's trying to make everything as festive as possible, even with, well, you know."

I definitely knew. And even though I was sure Jackie knew almost as much as we did about the case—you couldn't run a business that had a good percentage of the town's population coming through on a regular basis without learning about every single thing of note that was happening in Globe—that didn't mean I thought we should talk about it openly.

"That's good," I said, glad that Archie knew how he should be treating his soon-to-be wife. Not that I expected any less of him, considering how besotted he was with Victoria, but still, after so many years of not thinking he would ever fall in love with anyone, and many more years trapped in a cat's body, this whole world of romance was still fairly new for him.

Jackie came by with Victoria's glass of chardonnay, confirmed that all of us wanted French manicures, and then sent over three technicians to start working on us. I had to admit it felt good to have someone do my toes and rub my feet, since it had been a while since my last pedicure. Hazel also looked as though she was enjoying herself, taking sips of chardonnay, dipping into the conversation when we started discussing the music for the reception.

"So, you decided to rent a dance floor after all?" she asked.

"Just a small one," Victoria replied. "The backyard is big, but it's not *that* big. But I knew Archie wanted to have a first dance, and there's enough room that about half the people coming should be able to fit as long as they don't get too crazy."

Somehow, I doubted anyone attending the wedding would turn the dance floor into a mosh pit. It would be a small group, just twenty-five of us, which Victoria had said suited her just fine.

"I've overseen enough huge weddings that I'm fine with having something small and low-key," she'd told me months ago when she and Archie were still in the early planning stages of the ceremony, and I could totally understand her position. Calvin's and my wedding had ballooned into a much bigger production than I'd originally planned, partly because his own family was so large, and although I wouldn't have changed a single thing about the day, I also had to admit it had been kind of exhausting.

Then again, a good chunk of weariness at the end of that particular day could have been because I'd been up past midnight the evening before making sure Alice Bigelow, the resident ghost in the mansion where the wedding had taken place, was finally reunited with her true love and able to move on to the next plane of existence.

Victoria would have her parents at her ceremony, although the rest of her family back in Minnesota wouldn't be attending, mostly because her brothers and sister all had small children to wrangle. The other guests included a couple of her college sorority sisters, and some friends she'd made while living here in Globe.

One of whom was Joyce Lewis, who obviously would bring Henry with her.

That wouldn't be awkward at all.

As best I could, though, I pushed all that out of my head, and tried to focus on how lovely the day would be despite Victoria's current legal troubles. After all, it could have been worse—the judge could have denied bail, could have told Victoria she needed to put everything on hold until after the trial. I still wasn't thrilled with him for keeping her here instead of allowing her to go on her honeymoon, but it was still better than being behind bars.

The spa day—such as it was—had been my treat, so I headed up to the counter with Jackie so I could pay for all three of our mani/pedis. When I handed one of my debit cards to her, however, the card machine made an extremely unpleasant sound.

"I'm so sorry," Jackie said, not quite meeting my eyes. "Your card was declined."

Declined? I thought, flabbergasted. No, I didn't check my accounts every day, but I knew there had to be at least fifty thousand dollars in the one that particular card was attached to. There was no way in the world there couldn't be enough to cover the two hundred bucks or so that our three manicures and pedicures had cost.

Trying to ignore the unpleasant *thump-thump* of my worried heart, I pulled out another card. "Try this one."

To my infinite relief, that one went through, and because Victoria and Hazel had been taking their time slipping their sandals back on, I didn't think they'd noticed anything. I forced a smile as they approached the counter.

"I guess we'll all reconvene at Victoria's house tomorrow," I said, and she nodded.

"That's the plan," she said. "See you around ten-thirty?"

We'd already agreed on that hour—I could tell she didn't want Hazel and me coming over too early—so I just nodded. "See you then."

Hazel also promised to be there at ten-thirty, and we all got into our separate vehicles and headed home.

The whole way, my thoughts wouldn't stop racing, trying to figure out what had gone wrong with my debit card. True, that wasn't my biggest account, and I had literally millions of dollars stashed in various places, some of which were investment accounts that would be very difficult to access, but still.

What the hell was going on?

Calvin was already home from work, and he

took one look at my face as I rushed into the house and said, "What's wrong? Did something happen at your appointment?"

"They declined my card, is what happened," I told him, and his dark eyes widened in shock.

"That's impossible."

His tone was flat; while he'd always told me the money I'd inherited from Lucien Dumond was mine and he didn't have any right to any of it, he still knew enough to realize there was no way even the smallest of my accounts wouldn't have sufficient funds to cover a trip to the nail salon.

"We'd better go look," I told him.

So the two of us headed into my office, Sadie dancing at our heels and looking puzzled why we'd gone straight there rather than settling down in the living room or going to the kitchen the way we normally would. I booted up my laptop and logged into my account...only to find, as my stomach clenched in shock, that it had been drained down to almost nothing, with only a hundred dollars and some change left.

Just enough so I wouldn't have gotten a warning text from the bank, letting me know I'd fallen below the minimum I'd set for any account balance alerts.

It wasn't as though the money had been taken out in one lump sum, though. No, there were dozens and dozens of charges, mostly to online jewelry and electronics stores, some to clothing and shoe outlets.

"I didn't even realize you could spend eight thousand dollars at Zappos," Calvin remarked as he looked over my shoulder.

"Oh, you'd be surprised," I said. "I mean, one pair of Fluevog boots is like five hundred bucks or something. But I know I sure as hell didn't spend any of this."

"You need to call the bank and report all these fraudulent transactions," my husband replied. "And then try to find out where all this stuff is being shipped. That should point you toward the thief."

That sounded like a great idea—except I'd already promised Victoria all my time over the next couple of days, and there was no way I'd be able to call all the various outlets and try to convince them I needed to know where those items were going.

I explained as much to Calvin, then added, "But I'll call the bank and lock down the account, and then I'll follow up on all this other stuff after the wedding."

"Better lock down all your accounts," he responded, his expression grim. "We don't know how this person was able to access the one, and they might try to go after your other ones, too."

So that was why I spent the next two hours on

the phone, making sure I'd be contacted if anyone tried to charge anything over a hundred dollars on any of those accounts. Luckily, Calvin still had his own separate checking account, the one he'd had before we got together, and there was plenty of money in it to cover bills and any other household expenses that might crop up before we could get this whole mess straightened out.

By the time I was done, I felt as if I'd been run over by a truck repeatedly, so Calvin made me a comfort meal of grilled cheese and tomato soup, and we went into the living room to watch TV afterward, with my head pillowed on his shoulder and Sadie curled at my feet. That evidence of domestic tranquility made me feel a little better... but not all the way.

Just who had broken into my accounts, and how?

Worry about it later, I told myself. *You've done your due diligence, and now you need to focus on Archie and Victoria.*

All the same, I knew I'd be very glad when the entire event was safely over with.

16

Taking the Plunge

I'D ALREADY RESOLVED NOT TO SAY A WORD about the theft from my checking account to either Archie or Victoria, or even Hazel. Unburdening myself wouldn't change anything, and it was far more important to me that my friends could enjoy their special day, even if none of us could quite ignore that this wasn't the wedding they'd been planning for all these months.

Part of the reason Victoria had wanted me at the house around ten-thirty was that the party supply company was supposed to show up at eleven to deliver the chairs and tables for the backyard reception. True to form, the delivery people arrived half an hour early, which meant I'd barely gotten there in enough time to start directing traffic. Hazel was nowhere to be seen, but that didn't bother me too much. I loved her to death, but she often wasn't the most punctual person in the world, especially when something involved her showing up before noon. How she dealt with being married to a rancher, someone who needed to be up at dawn most of the time, I had absolutely no idea.

Once I got the delivery drama handled—Victoria had been on the phone with the caterer and Archie was off picking up his suit, which had needed a couple of last-minute alterations—Hazel arrived, a portfolio tucked under one arm and her box of paints in her other hand.

"Did I miss much?" she asked.

Part of me wanted to make a sarcastic comment about how nice it was to see her—she was almost a half hour late by that point—but I bit my tongue. I knew I was on edge because of the mysterious draining of that one bank account, and going off on Hazel for being Hazel would have been pointless.

"Not a lot," I said. "But now that you're here, we can start setting up the chairs for the ceremony."

She sent me a dubious look. "Shouldn't you wait until Archie can help with that?"

"He's off picking up his suit," I said. "And I'm only four months pregnant. I can manage. It's not like we're moving an entire house full of furniture or something."

She opened her mouth, as though to make at least a half-hearted protest, then appeared to think better of it, because she only nodded and said, "Okay."

We spent the next fifteen minutes arranging the chairs in three rows of five on either side, leaving ample room for the aisle that Victoria would walk down. The flowers wouldn't arrive until tomorrow morning, when there would be a mad rush to get them all set up and in their proper places, but for now, it was enough to make sure the chairs were ready to go, as well as the small dance floor that had been laid down over to one side.

"That looks good," Hazel said once we were done, looking over the setup with a critical eye. "But now I need to get started on the reception book. Archie and Victoria just finally decided on their design last night."

"Are you going to have enough time?" I asked, thinking she was cutting it a little close.

"Oh, sure," she said easily. "I'm using watercolors, so they'll dry fast. It's not like I'm doing a massive oil painting or something."

A while back, Hazel had suggested that she paint a custom cover for their reception book, something that would make it unique and utterly unlike anything they could have bought commercially. Both Victoria and Archie had said that sounded like a wonderful idea, and I had to admit I thought it was pretty cool, too.

In fact, I'd even needled Hazel about it, asking her why she hadn't done something like that for Calvin's and my wedding, but she'd only shrugged, saying she'd just heard about it in an artists' forum where she hung out, so it wasn't like she could have painted one for me.

I'd accepted that explanation and hadn't thought much about it after that. However, just like too many other pieces of this wedding puzzle, the reception book sounded as if it had gotten pushed to the very last minute.

"I'm going to use the kitchen table for my workspace," she told me. "I figure I'll be out of the way, but close by in case you need me for something."

"Well, now that we have the chairs set up, there isn't a whole lot for me to do until the caterer drops off their stuff," I replied. "Or at least, the things that are coming today. The cake and some other bits and pieces have to be delivered tomorrow morning."

She nodded, and took her supplies and the reception book over to the kitchen table, which I had to admit was a great spot for that kind of work, with its wide surface and the natural light that came pouring in through the large window next to it.

I was just wondering if I should go in search of Victoria—it seemed as if she'd been on the phone with the caterer for an awfully long time—when she appeared at the kitchen door, nose wrinkled.

"Do you know if one of the delivery guys used the downstairs bathroom?"

"I'm not sure," I replied. "There were a bunch of people coming and going, and I couldn't keep track of all of them."

She let out a disgusted breath. "Well, the toilet's all backed up."

Yuck. Probably one of the last things you wanted to deal with on the eve of your wedding day. "Do you have a plunger?"

"No," she said. "We've never needed one before now."

Hazel, who'd just finished setting out her little palette of watercolors, looked over at us and said, "I have one at my Airbnb. It's a lot closer than having to run over to Walmart."

And definitely closer than having to drive to either Hazel's or my house, both of which were located outside Globe's town limits.

Victoria raised an eyebrow. "I thought Selena's new assistant was staying there."

"She is," I said, even though Victoria had been addressing Hazel rather than me. "But she's at work right now, watching the shop for me. Why don't I call her and see if it's okay if I can go borrow it?"

Because it made much more sense for me to run the errand, since Hazel was busy with painting the cover of the reception book, and Victoria really needed to stay put to intercept any other deliveries that might arrive today.

"Oh, would you?" Victoria asked, looking much relieved. "I really need to know if it's something that can be fixed easily, or whether I need to call a plumber. We've only got the one bathroom downstairs, and I can't have it out of commission with a house full of people coming over tomorrow."

"Not a problem," I said, and went over to the spot where I'd left my purse on the kitchen counter so I could get out my phone and make the call. The phone rang twice, and then Melanie picked up.

"Once in a Blue Moon."

"Hi, Melanie," I said. "It's Selena. I wanted to know if it was okay if I popped over to your Airbnb and got the plunger from the bathroom. It's kind of an emergency."

"Um…sure," she replied, sounding a little startled. "I think it's tucked behind the toilet."

"I'll find it," I told her. "How's everything going at the shop?"

"Just fine," she said. "Quiet so far. Do you need me to meet you over there?"

"No, it's okay," I replied. "Hazel still has a key, so I'm going to use that."

Maybe there was the faintest pause as Melanie appeared to absorb my reply. Had she forgotten that she hadn't signed a real lease on the cottage yet, and therefore of course Hazel would have a key?

Hard to say, because after that very brief hesitation, Melanie said, "Oh, sure. Then yeah, go ahead and get it. I hope that will solve your problem."

"Me too," I said. Considering everything else Victoria was juggling at the moment, she really didn't need to deal with a plumber's bill—assuming she could even get someone out here that quickly—on top of everything else.

I thanked Melanie and ended the call, then turned back toward Hazel. "The key?"

"Right here." She set down her paintbrush and dug a set of keys out of her jeans pocket. "It's the one with the fox design on it."

Sure enough, all of Hazel's keys were as colorful as the palettes she used in her paintings, with flowers and rainbows and, as described, an adorable pale blue one with an orange fox head on it.

"Got it," I said. I glanced over at Victoria and added, "I'll be as fast as I can."

"Thank you so much."

I told her it wasn't a problem, then hurried out and got into my Renegade. Technically, the cottage was within walking distance from Victoria and Archie's house, but that would have taken twice as long as driving, and time was of the essence.

Hazel's Airbnb looked just the same as it always had, although some flowers in the beds were starting to appear a little tired, as if they knew their winter sleep was coming up fast. Keys in hand, I mounted the front steps and went inside.

Although I'd spent plenty of time here before she moved in with Chuck, something about the place felt different now. It could have been that some of her personal artwork had been removed from the walls and replaced with more generic canvas prints, but I thought it was something more than that, as if the essence of Hazel that had once existed here was now long gone and nothing had ever taken its place, since the cottage had seen a not-quite-steady stream of vacationers since she left.

But at least it looked neat and clean enough, and I was glad to learn that Melanie wasn't secretly a slob or something. True, there were worse character traits, but I'd always had a kind of a low opinion of people who trashed hotel rooms or apartments, and basically showed disdain for the places they were renting.

Because the cottage was almost as familiar to me as the flat I'd once lived in over the store, I knew its single bathroom was in the middle of a short hall off the living room, between the main bedroom and a secondary space that Hazel had once used as a studio but was now decorated as a children's room with two twin beds, making the little house a good choice for vacationers with kids. I headed straight for that bathroom and moved past the vanity, my gaze already landing on the plunger where it was almost hidden behind the toilet.

I hurried over and wrapped my fingers around the wooden handle, then paused. In the trash can on the other side of the toilet, a brightly colored box caught my eye. Looking closer, I saw it was a box of hair color—L'Óreal Light Ash Brown, to be exact.

On the surface, finding a box of hair color didn't seem like that big a deal. Maybe Melanie was prematurely gray, or maybe she just didn't like her natural shade and used something to spice it up a bit.

But....

All of my hedgewitch senses were tingling,

and I knew in my gut there had to be a much less innocent reason for Melanie wanting to change her hair color.

Grandma Ellen's words echoed in my mind.

The answer to your question isn't as far away as you might think.

Had she been trying to tell me that Melanie Knowles was the person who'd murdered Jeffrey Sellers?

After all, if she was trying to hide her identity, then coloring her bright blonde hair a nondescript brown was probably a good place to start.

I didn't know why Melanie would have gotten a job at the store, though. Was it only because she needed access to Victoria's studio, and being right there had seemed the easiest way to go about it? After all, the same key opened both the door to the shop and her studio—we'd set it up that way because it was just easier, and we knew we could trust each other with our property.

And...I kept that key in the cash register during business hours. It would have been way too easy for Melanie to grab the key while I was taking a bathroom break and head upstairs to pour that atropine into the creamer in Victoria's fridge.

No wonder the police hadn't detected any signs of forced entry.

My hands began to shake, and I forced myself

to take a deep breath. Right now, I only had a theory, and I knew I was going to need a lot more than that to convince Henry he needed to arrest Melanie Knowles for Jeffrey Sellers' murder.

And the only way to get that evidence was to force a confession out of my would-be assistant.

I hurried out of the bathroom, pausing just long enough to lock the front door, then practically ran to my Renegade where it was parked at the curb. For just a moment, I thought about heading straight to the shop, but then I remembered Victoria was waiting for me.

Cursing under my breath, I pointed the Jeep toward her house and took the front steps two at a time. I rang the doorbell, waited, and then all but threw the plunger at Victoria when she opened the door.

"Here you go," I said breathlessly. "But I just thought of something I need to do at the store. I'll be back as soon as I can."

She frowned. "Is everything okay?"

"Sure," I said quickly. "I hope the plunger works out!"

Before she could reply, I'd already turned and was running back down the steps to my car. Once inside, I practically had the poor Jeep leap away from the curb as my foot hit the accelerator, although I made myself slow down once I was off her street, telling myself that getting pulled over for speeding wouldn't help my situation any.

As I drove, I tried to rehearse what I would say to Melanie. Should I go with a straight-up accusation, or should I try to circle around to the subject and hope she might drop a few incriminating comments all on her own?

The direct approach was probably best. She'd been smart enough to pull the wool over my eyes for the past week, so I had no reason to believe she would say anything that would give up the game without my goading her into it.

And I knew I was going on a hunch, and that maybe I was absolutely dead wrong about all this. After all, with my spells and my magic currently being checked by the baby's "medicine," how could I be sure I was right?

Okay, little one, I thought as I pulled into the parking lot behind the shop. *If you could let me see my auras for even a minute, that would be an enormous help. At least then, I'd know I haven't gone crazy.*

Because I knew if I was wrong about all this, there was no way I'd be able to keep Melanie as my assistant. Usually, people cut ties with anyone who wrongly accused them of murder...and who could blame them?

I also knew I was taking a huge chance coming here alone. The thought had crossed my mind that I should call Calvin and tell him what I had planned, ask him to come provide backup, but it would take him at least twenty minutes to get to town, and even then, I didn't know whether having him here was a very good idea. Jeffrey Sellers' murder had taken place firmly in Chief Lewis's jurisdiction, and I knew he was not a fan of having my husband butt in.

But there wasn't any reason why I couldn't let Henry know what I was doing…as long as I got him to promise he wouldn't intercede until I'd managed to have Melanie spill the beans.

Long ago, I'd programmed the Globe police department's number in my phone, so it was easy enough to make a quick call while I was parked there, all the while praying that Melanie wouldn't take that exact moment to come out and put the trash in the dumpster behind the building.

"Hi, Loretta," I said when the deputy at the reception desk answered the phone with her usual spiel about asking whether this was an emergency. "I need to talk to Henry. Is he in his office?"

"Yes," she replied, her tone guarded. It wasn't that Loretta and I didn't get along, but more that she knew if I was calling to talk to her boss, then something must be going down. "Can I tell him why you're calling?"

"Just let him know I have some information about the Jeffrey Sellers murder investigation."

She made a clicking sound with her tongue, and told me she needed to put me on hold for a minute. Less than thirty seconds later, Henry's voice came through my iPhone's speaker.

"What's this about, Selena?"

"I think I might have cracked the case," I said. "You need to stay on the phone and listen, and then decide if you need to intervene."

"'Intervene'?" he repeated, sounding incredulous. "What are you talking about?"

"Just listen," I told him. "But don't say anything, or you're going to blow the whole thing."

After delivering that command, I slid the phone into my skirt pocket rather than returning it to my purse, since I figured the lightweight fabric of my skirt wouldn't muffle my conversation with Melanie the way hiding in a compartment in my purse might. Doing my best to act calm, I got out of my car, locked it, and then came in through the little back lobby and into Once in a Blue Moon.

Everything seemed quiet enough, with only the faint New Age music I always had playing in the store's background to break up the stillness. If there were any customers, they must have been silently browsing rather than asking Melanie for help.

In fact, when I moved past the door to the

stockroom and the bathroom, it was to find the shop completely empty except for my assistant, who was scrolling through something on her phone.

Irritation stabbed through me. How typical that she'd be on her phone as soon as I wasn't around to supervise.

Almost immediately, I told myself not to be an idiot, that Melanie's job performance was pretty far down the list of things I needed to be worrying about right now.

As I stared at her, though, I realized she looked different. About a second later, my brain cells kicked in, and I knew exactly why.

I was seeing her aura.

It was a murky brownish red, like soil soaked with blood. Here and there were flashes of brighter red and an extremely unpleasant dark yellow that reminded me of the crust that formed on a mustard bottle when it hadn't been wiped down properly.

If that wasn't the aura of a woman who'd murdered a man in cold blood, I didn't know what was.

I didn't have time to wonder how or why my auras had come back—had my unborn child heard my plea and decided to take pity on me?—but I decided that didn't matter.

What mattered was that Melanie's aura was as

much a sign of her guilt as any confession could be.

However, Henry Lewis needed evidence, not auras that only I could see.

She glanced up from her phone, and her eyes widened. "Selena?" she said. "Couldn't you find the plunger?"

"No, I found it, Melanie," I said, clearly stating her name so Henry would know exactly who I was speaking to. "And I already took it over to Victoria's house. But I wanted to talk to you about something else I found."

Melanie's expression was almost blank, as if she was doing some rapid mental calculations in order to figure out if I could have seen something incriminating at the cottage. Obviously, she could have no idea that I'd already guessed—and gotten backup from the pendulum and my Tarot cards—that Jeffrey Sellers' murderer was blonde, and therefore that the box of L'Óreal hair dye in her trash was a lot more suspicious than she could have known.

"I was in a rush when I left the house this morning," she said. "So I didn't have time to put my breakfast dishes away. I wasn't aware Hazel had a problem with her guests not keeping everything perfect all the time."

A definite snotty note had crept into Melanie's tone, something I hadn't yet heard from her. Of course not—she'd been pretending to be all sweetness and light, and would have worked very, very hard to keep me from learning anything about her true personality.

Honestly, I hadn't even gone near the kitchen, so I couldn't really comment on its cleanliness...or lack thereof.

"No, that's not it," I said. "It's about that box of hair dye I found in the bathroom."

"So?" she returned, the challenge clear in her voice. "I wasn't aware it was against the law to color your hair."

"It's not," I said coolly. "But it's kind of a problem when you're using it to hide your identity, to make sure no one would connect you with the blonde woman who was seen coming and going from Jeffrey Sellers' apartment."

For a long moment, Melanie just stared at me, her expression again almost too blank. Then she gave a forced laugh and responded, "I don't know what you're talking about, Selena. Are you feeling okay? Maybe you need to sit down."

The condescension in her tone was clear. Obviously, she was trying to make me think I was some addled pregnant woman, someone who had so many hormones swirling around in her brain, she didn't know what was going on.

Too bad she had no idea who she was dealing with.

"No, I'm fine," I said, my voice equally cool. "It's so obvious, Melanie—you wanted a job here so you'd have easy access to Victoria's studio and could put that atropine in the creamer. You knew Jeffrey would ask for it, and you knew he'd die quickly, before anyone could even try to intervene. But I'm curious why you would go to those lengths. Did you want a bigger cut of the money?"

She was shaking her head, still trying to look calm, but I could tell from the flash of panic in her eyes that I'd latched on to at least part of the truth. "You're really talking crazy, Selena. Do you want me to call Calvin? It sounds like you need to lie down. Maybe all the fuss around Archie and Victoria's wedding has been stressing you out too much."

Oh, I was stressed, all right...but not because of the wedding. No, it was more that I'd really been hoping Melanie would drop the ball somewhere, would blurt out something that would be the one convincing piece of evidence that would tell Henry it was time to swoop in and slap the cuffs on her.

I smiled, doing my best to show that her little psychological jabs wouldn't make a bit of difference. "And you knew about Sara Tilden and NancyAnne Nielsen, didn't you? That's why you wanted to make sure you used a poison that only someone in the healthcare field would have access to. I'm curious how you were able to get your hands on some, though."

Melanie's eyes narrowed. "I don't know either of those women. I don't know—"

She never got to finish the sentence, because Henry Lewis and one of his deputies burst into the store right then and made a beeline for her. I had to give her credit for fast reflexes—she took one look at them and knocked over a stand filled with postcards and pocket calendars, then bolted for the back entrance.

Luckily, though, Henry was able to dodge the postcard avalanche and caught hold of one of her wrists, yanking her back toward him. As she let out a little cry of pain, he pulled off the handcuffs hanging from his belt and slapped them on her.

"Melanie Knowles," he said, "I'm arresting you for the murder of Jeffrey Sellers."

17

Honor Among Thieves

"But how did you know?" I asked Henry, after his deputy had carted Melanie away to get booked at the police station.

The police chief was looking pretty pleased with himself, and I couldn't really blame him. "It was when you mentioned Sara Tilden and Nancy-Anne Nielsen being in the healthcare industry. I ran a quick check on Melanie Knowles and discovered that she's actually an RN who works at Chandler Regional Medical Center."

"She's a nurse?" I said, knowing how shocked I sounded. "But she told me she worked in retail."

Henry's gray eyes glinted at me, amused. "You're a trusting soul, Selena."

I hated the implication that I was some kind of naïve idiot who couldn't even be bothered to check a prospective employee's references. "I called the places she worked," I told him. "They confirmed her employment."

"They were probably friends of hers that she roped into pretending to be former bosses," he said. "Did you actually cross-reference those numbers against the numbers listed for those stores online?"

Oops. That was something I definitely hadn't done…mostly because it would never have occurred to me to take checking Melanie's references to such lengths.

"It's okay," he went on, while I stood there in flummoxed silence. "Most people don't go to that much trouble when checking references. On the surface, Ms. Knowles probably looked perfect to you."

That was for sure. Should I be kicking myself for thinking no one could have been so exactly tailored to the kind of person I needed to take over at the store?

Well, I'd put aside the self-recriminations until later. Right now, I had more important things to worry about.

"So…what happens to Victoria now?" I asked.

Henry gave me a very small smile. "Oh, I'm going to go to the station and see if Ms. Knowles has anything she wants to tell me. Probably, she'll clam up, but I'll still see the D.A. and let him know we have a suspect in custody and that all the charges against Victoria Parrish need to be dropped. He might push back a little, but I'm pretty sure he'll let it go, since he'll have a much more viable prospect for prosecution in Melanie Knowles."

Those words couldn't make me relax all the way, and yet I had to believe Henry knew what he was talking about, and that now all any of us could do was wait to get the all-clear from the district attorney.

In the meantime, though, I needed to get back to Victoria's house.

I was going to have quite the story to tell.

Hazel and Victoria—and Archie, too, since he'd returned from his trip to the tailor during my absence—listened to me, wide-eyed, as I explained why I'd taken off like that after delivering the plunger.

"You figured it out just by looking at a box of hair dye?" Archie inquired, sounding almost but not quite skeptical.

Since I'd been expecting that kind of response from him, I only shrugged. "Women's intuition," I said. "Well, that and realizing the woman we'd been looking for was blonde, but there weren't any newcomers in Globe who fit that description. It made total sense to me that Melanie had been coloring her hair to throw people off the scent... but was also using a demi-permanent color that washed out easily so it would be easier to go back to blonde when she was done with all this. Otherwise, she wouldn't have needed to re-color it again so soon."

And that was probably why she'd also chosen a shade that would fade easily. If she'd gone for bright red or dark brown, it would have been a lot harder to go back to her original color once she was done playing shop assistant.

"I'm sure we'll hear more of the story after Henry questions her," Hazel said. "But for now, it looks like you're off the hook, Victoria."

"Well, almost," I cautioned. "Henry didn't really give me a timeline for when he thought the D.A. would drop the charges."

At that exact moment, Victoria's phone rang from inside her purse. She excused herself, then went to get it and put it to her ear. "Victoria Parrish."

She was quiet as the person calling seemed to respond at length. During that time, though, the slightly worried, distracted expression she'd been wearing shifted into one I could only describe as pure joy.

Eventually, she said, "Yes, I understand. Thank you so much for calling to let me know."

And then she lowered the phone and stood there for a second, as if she wasn't quite sure what she was supposed to do next.

"Well?" Hazel prompted, while Archie went over to take Victoria by the hand, his expression also questioning.

"That was the district attorney," she said, smiling. "All the charges against me have been dropped." Her fingers tightened on Archie's, and she added, "We can go on our honeymoon!"

He stared at her incredulously for a second, and then pulled her into his arms, kissing her so passionately that I guessed he'd completely forgotten they had an audience.

Which was fine. The only important thing was that it looked as though the two of them would get their happy ending after all.

There were still a million odds and ends to be handled—although the plunger had done the trick, thank the Goddess—but at three o'clock the following afternoon, Archie and Victoria's friends and family gathered in their backyard on a picture-perfect October day, and watched the two of them become husband and wife.

The expression Archie wore as he kissed his beautiful bride was almost incredulous, as if he still couldn't quite figure out how he'd managed to get such an exquisite creature to become his wife. But she kissed him back, smiling, their hands clasped in one another's, and the reality of it seemed to sink in, that despite all the tribulations he'd suffered, he'd survived to come to this place, to have Victoria at his side in the gracious home they'd bought together.

I'd never met Victoria's parents before since they lived in Minnesota and had only come to Arizona to see their daughter married, but the two of them seemed wonderful, friendly and down-to-earth—and, I thought, very relieved to see the last of their children married off to someone they apparently thought was just perfect for her.

"Don't they look amazing together?" Victoria's mother, Jenny, whispered to me as the newlyweds cut their cake later at the reception. "Like a couple of movie stars or something."

Since I'd privately thought Victoria and Archie could have stood in for a pair of celebrities from Hollywood's golden age, I didn't disagree with that assessment one bit. "They do make a beautiful couple," I whispered back. "I'm so happy for them."

"Me too," Jenny said, and blinked back some fond tears. "Me too."

A little later, I was dancing with Archie—a slow waltz, since I'd told him I didn't want to do anything more vigorous—and I commented, "Your new in-laws seem to approve of you."

"And you're surprised by that?" he returned, although the slight smile he wore told me he hadn't been offended by my words.

"Not at all," I said smoothly. "I'm just glad for you…for all of you."

He inclined his head, and we danced in silence for a few moments. Then he said, "I don't think I've thanked you properly for coming to Victoria's rescue. That was quite something, figuring out Melanie Knowles was the real murderer."

"Well, I had help," I said. "Henry's really the one who saved the day."

"Perhaps," Archie allowed. "Either way, it means Victoria and I don't have to worry about what's coming next, and that we can leave for California in the morning and know all of this mess is safely behind us."

I only nodded. It was true that my friends deserved to sail off into the sunset to enjoy themselves in Napa.

But I…

…well, I still had a lot of questions that needed to be answered.

Calvin wasn't too thrilled about my plan to visit Melanie Knowles in jail, although he also didn't try to talk me out of it.

"Do you even think Henry will let you see her?" he asked.

We were both in the bathroom, getting ready for our Monday morning. On Sunday, we'd mostly just lazed around the house, recovering from the wedding, although I'd gotten myself together enough to investigate some of the bigger fraudulent purchases on my debit card, and had discovered they'd all been sent to the same address in Chandler.

Not Melanie Knowles' apartment…she would never have been that careless…but to a mailbox at a UPS store not too far from where she lived.

It would have been easy enough for her. All she had to do was wait until I was taking a bath-room break, then slip the cards out of my wallet and write down the numbers, expiration dates, and security codes. After that, she would be free to go on an online shopping spree at my expense.

True, she'd been taking a risk, but she'd prob-ably thought I didn't use that particular card and its attached account very often, since my other three debit cards had been stacked on top of it. And she also might have thought that I'd be way too occupied with Archie and Victoria's wedding

—and Victoria's court case—to have time to check my account balances.

Melanie probably would have gotten away with it…if I hadn't used that one card to pay for the wedding party's appointment at the nail salon.

Because, after she was arrested and Henry and his deputies searched the Airbnb to see if they could find any more evidence to use in the case against her, they'd found Melanie's bags packed and ready to go. It seemed pretty obvious to everyone involved that she'd planned to clear out as soon as she was done covering my shift at the store on Saturday. Because we were closed on Sundays and I wouldn't have had any reason to be in touch with her until Monday morning, she would have been long gone.

And although she had probably been itching to get out of here sooner rather than later, leaving before the end of the day on Saturday would have been too obvious. All it would have taken was for one person to call me and ask why the store was closed on a day when it should have been open, and the jig would have been up for sure.

"Oh, I'm pretty sure Henry will let me talk to Melanie," I said as I leaned forward to brush on some mascara. "After all, I know he wouldn't have even considered her a suspect if it weren't for me."

Calvin made a noncommittal sound, but at least he didn't offer any further protests…just as he hadn't protested when I'd instructed my accountant to send NancyAnne Nielsen a cashier's check for fifty thousand dollars. No, I didn't have any obligation to take care of her, and yet I couldn't get her pinched, worried expression out of my mind, or the cracked screen of an iPhone that was way past its expiration date.

I hoped the money would give her a chance at a much better life than the one Jeffrey Sellers had promised her.

Calvin and I both left the house at around the same time that Monday morning, even though he had to be at the station at nine and I didn't need to open the doors to Once in a Blue Moon until an hour later. I drove past the shop and pulled into the parking lot at Globe's police station, a place I'd gotten way more familiar with over the past couple of years than I'd ever thought I would.

In fact, Henry was at the front desk when I came in, a cup of coffee in one hand while he chatted with Loretta Stillman, who occupied her usual post behind that desk. As soon as he caught sight of me, his lip curled slightly.

"I assume this isn't a social visit?"

"Not really," I said. "I was hoping I could talk to Melanie."

"You're not going to get anything out of her," he replied, now looking annoyed—not at me, but at his recalcitrant prisoner. "She's lawyered up and isn't talking. Her prerogative, but I doubt she's going to suddenly open up just because you're there."

"Maybe not," I allowed. "Still, I'd like the chance. I won't take too long—I need to get over to the shop after this."

A shop I'd have to go back to running on my own, since my new hire had turned out to be a murderer.

Henry hesitated for a moment...but only a moment. Then he said, "If you want to waste your time, go right ahead. Let me take you back there."

He set his cup of coffee on Loretta's desk, then gestured at me to follow him toward the rear of the station, where the holding cells were located. This wasn't my first time back here, but they hadn't improved with age, were still dark and gray and definitely not intended for comfort. A couple of those cells were occupied by people I guessed had been pulled over for traffic violations and then discovered to have a little more alcohol in their systems than the State of Arizona allowed a person behind the wheel.

The cell at the very end—with several empty ones in between hers and the ones that contained people who obviously hadn't been able to make bail—held Melanie Knowles. She wore an orange prison jumpsuit and had her hair pulled back in a plain ponytail, but otherwise, it didn't seem as if her experience had affected her too much. One eyebrow went up as I approached, and that was the only reaction I got.

"I'll be back in fifteen minutes," Henry said, ignoring her and facing me. "But if you get done before then, I assume you can find your way back to the front desk."

"Yes, I know the way," I said with a grin.

His mouth tightened in disapproval, but he didn't say anything, just nodded and headed toward the front of the station, leaving me alone with Melanie.

To my surprise, she spoke as soon as he was gone. "I suppose you've been patting yourself on the back all weekend."

"Not really," I replied, gazing back at her. There didn't seem to be much evidence of guilt or even worry in her expression. Instead, she looked more amused than anything else. "I mean, I was stupid enough to hire you in the first place, right?"

Her shoulders lifted. "Oh, I made sure you would, once I realized what a perfect opening you'd given me. That was a great resume, wasn't it?"

"It was," I admitted, even as I inwardly gritted my teeth. Judging by the faint smile she wore, it seemed pretty obvious to me that she was extremely amused by the way I'd walked right into her trap. "And the references? Friends of yours?"

"Yes," she said. "It was way too easy to set up. I mean, I was pretty sure I didn't have to worry about you doing a background check like I was applying for a security clearance or something."

I definitely hadn't done anything like that. No, I'd assumed she was on the up and up, and that calling a couple of her references was all I had to do.

Big mistake.

"So...why?" I asked then. "Why kill Jeffrey Sellers?"

At once, her expression shut down. "I'm afraid I'm not at liberty to discuss the details of my case."

That definitely sounded like something her lawyer had told her to say. "Was it because you found out about Sara Tilden, or maybe Jeffrey's ex-wife?"

Melanie's mouth flattened. "I'm not saying anything. Don't you have a store you need to open up? I mean, now that you have to handle the whole thing by yourself, I'd think you would need extra time."

What a —

I pushed the thought away as soon as it popped up. Mentally calling Melanie Knowles names wasn't going to change the situation, especially since it was pretty obvious that she had no more intention of talking to me than she did to the police.

Instead, I stepped forward, smiled, and said, "Better get used to those bars, Melanie."

And then I turned and walked away.

Of course, all the sordid details eventually came out, even though Melanie had refused to testify at her own trial, and all the evidence against her was information dug up by the district attorney's office. By that point, it was almost December, and I was nearly six months pregnant…and no closer to finding someone to help me out at the shop than I'd been before Melanie arrived on the scene.

Once burned, twice shy, I supposed.

Anyway, it turned out that Melanie and Jeffrey had cooked up the plan to blackmail Archie after Jeffrey began digging into Archie's background and found a few inconsistencies that he wanted to exploit. Luckily, the D.A. didn't go too much into that, so my friend's secrets remained secret, but it established a motive.

But then Jeffrey apparently let slip to Melanie that he planned to hand over a chunk of the blackmail money to NancyAnne Nielsen in order to pay off his back child support, and she seemed to decide she didn't need him and would rather keep it all for herself, a not unreasonable decision to make, I supposed, considering she had almost a hundred grand of credit card debt thanks to her over-the-top shopping habits. She talked him into approaching Victoria, while at the same time answering my ad so she'd be close enough to assess the situation and figure out the best way to proceed.

Slipping the atropine into the creamer had been easy enough; she'd stolen the drug from a locker at the hospital where she worked—a hospital that hadn't even realized it was missing, or that she was doing a little more with the time off she'd requested than simply spending a few weeks in Cancun. And once Jeffrey was dead, she'd stuck around because she'd realized she'd found a much bigger mark, one she was all too happy to steal from.

Namely, me.

It sounded as though Melanie's plan had been to drain the other three accounts whose debit card information she'd also copied down. That would have given her hundreds of thousands of dollars in her pocket, plenty to allow her to disappear across the border and never get caught.

Except, of course, for the inconvenient way I'd discovered that my new assistant was much more than she'd pretended to be.

The jury had only deliberated for a single afternoon, and came back with a unanimous guilty verdict. And the day after that, the judge sentenced her to life in prison without the possibility of parole, meaning she was now cooling her heels at the maximum-security facility in Florence.

I had to wonder if she and Miriam Jacobsen, the former Globe Chamber of Commerce president who'd been sent there after being found guilty of being an accessory to murder, ever met in the prison yard and shared notes on how Selena Marx was the person who'd been instrumental in sending them to rot in prison.

Under other circumstances, I might have been worried about that. But this was real life, and I knew there was absolutely no chance of either of them getting out of the Florence facility any time soon. Miriam's sentence was much lighter, since she'd been an accessory to murder rather than the person who'd done the awful deed, but still, she had a good ten or so years to go before she could even think about applying for parole.

The day after the sentence was handed down, Calvin and I drove up into the mountains to cut down our holiday tree. It was a family tradition of his that we'd observed the first December after we were married, and I had to admit it was a little strange to think that next year, our child would share this same tradition with us.

"Feeling better?" he asked as he lent an arm to steady me as we made our way through the thick forest outside Payson.

I knew he wasn't talking about the morning sickness that had reared its ugly head this past week.

"Much better," I said. "It definitely helps to know that Melanie is locked up and far away from here."

He nodded. "That woman was a sociopath if I've ever seen one. Not a single hint of remorse."

That was for sure. Had she ever felt anything for Jeffrey Sellers, or was he only someone who'd been convenient to her for a while?

Hard to say, because, other than the bits and pieces the D.A. had pried out of her during the trial, she had said nothing else about the case.

"I can't believe she fooled me like that," I said, and Calvin gently pulled me to him so he could place a reassuring kiss on my cheek.

"Sounds like she fooled a lot of people," he replied. "So don't beat yourself up."

I nodded, since that was only the truth. No one had seemed to sense what she was capable of, the lengths she'd go to in order to get her hands on a big stack of cash. All I could do was thank the Goddess that my auras had come to my rescue, or I still might not have believed the kind of evil she'd harbored in her heart.

They'd come and gone since then, not entirely absent, but also not as frequent as they'd been before I'd gotten pregnant. Which was fine—it was good enough for me to know they weren't gone forever, and that they'd been there for me when I needed them.

"What about this one?" Calvin asked then, stopping in front of a perfect blue spruce. It was about six inches taller than he was, so just under seven feet in height, and perfectly proportioned.

"It's wonderful," I said, even as I told myself not to feel guilty about cutting down the pretty little tree. This area had already been tagged for thinning, and if we didn't cut it down, someone from the Forest Service would have come along and removed it, anyway. "It'll be perfect for that corner by the fireplace."

Calvin nodded and unhooked the axe he had hanging from his belt. With the ease of someone who'd done this many times before—after all, this had been a tradition in his own family, and one we were carrying on—he cut through the tree's trunk, then kneeled to tie it up with some twine so it would be easier to transport back to his Durango.

Even with the tree precariously balanced on one shoulder, he still held my hand as we made our way down the path to the trailhead where we'd parked the SUV. His fingers felt infinitely reassuring against mine, and I was happy in that moment, happy for the feel of the cold, fresh air against my cheeks, happy to know we were going back to the home we'd made together.

No more adventures, I vowed to myself. *This one was too close.*

I'd just have to see whether the universe would allow me to keep that promise.

Also by Christine Pope

FAMILIAR SPIRITS

(Cozy Mystery/Paranormal Romance)

Spells and Spaniels

Cauldrons and Cats

Hexes and Hedgehogs

Charms and Chihuahuas (March 2024)

LATTES AND LEVITATION

(Cozy Mystery/Paranormal Romance)

Caffeine Before Curses

Muffins After Magic

Pastries and Prophecies

Eclairs and Ectoplasm

Sugar Skulls and Specters

Wedding Cakes and Wishes (January 2024)

HEDGEWITCH FOR HIRE

(Cozy Mystery/Paranormal Romance)

Grave Mistake

Social Medium

Household Demons

Perpetual Potion

Jingle Spells

Wandering Monsters

Uninvited Ghosts

Prophet Motive

Ballroom Bits

Spell Check

Charm School (February 2024)

UNEXPECTED MAGIC*

(Urban Fantasy/Paranormal Romance)

Found Objects

Finders, Keepers

Lost and Found

Finding Destiny

THE WITCHES OF WHEELER PARK*

(Paranormal Romance)

Storm Born

Thunder Road

Winds of Change

Mind Games

A Wheeler Park Christmas

Blood Ties

Healing Hands

Wishful Thinking

Smoke and Mirrors

MISS PRIMM'S ACADEMY FOR WAYWARD
WITCHES*

(Fantasy/Academy Romance)

Misspelled

Dispelled

Expelled

PROJECT DEMON HUNTERS*

(Paranormal Romance)

Unquiet Souls

Unbound Spirits

Unholy Ground

Unseen Voices

Unmarked Graves

Unbroken Vows

THE DEVIL YOU KNOW*

(Paranormal Romance)

Sympathy for the Devil

Charmed, I'm Sure

A Wing and a Prayer

Wish Upon a Star

THE WITCHES OF CANYON ROAD*

(Paranormal Romance)

Hidden Gifts

Darker Paths

Mysterious Ways

A Canyon Road Christmas

Demon Born

An Ill Wind

Higher Ground

Haunted Hearts

THE WITCHES OF CLEOPATRA HILL*

(Paranormal Romance)

Darkangel

Darknight

Darkmoon

Sympathetic Magic

Protector

Spellbound

A Cleopatra Hill Christmas

Impractical Magic

Strange Magic

The Arrangement

Defender

Bad Blood

Deep Magic

Darktide

THE DJINN WARS*

(Paranormal Romance)

Chosen

Taken

Fallen

Broken

Forsaken

Forbidden

Awoken

Illuminated

Stolen

Forgotten

Driven

Unspoken

THE WATCHERS TRILOGY*

(Paranormal Romance)

Falling Dark

Dead of Night

Rising Dawn

THE SEDONA FILES*

(Paranormal/Science Fiction Romance)

Bad Vibrations

Desert Hearts

Angel Fire

Star Crossed

Falling Angels

Enemy Mine

TALES OF THE LATTER KINGDOMS*

(Fantasy Romance)

All Fall Down

Dragon Rose

Binding Spell

Ashes of Roses

One Thousand Nights

Threads of Gold

The Wolf of Harrow Hall

Moon Dance

The Song of the Thrush

THE GAIAN CONSORTIUM SERIES*

(Science Fiction Romance)

Beast (free prequel novella)

Blood Will Tell

Breath of Life

The Gaia Gambit

The Mandala Maneuver

The Titan Trap

The Zhore Deception

The Refugee Ruse

STANDALONE TITLES

Hearts on Fire (Paranormal Romance)

Taking Dictation (Contemporary Romance)

Golden Heart (Gaslight Fantasy Romance)

Night Music: A Modern Reimagining of The Phantom of the Opera (Contemporary Romance)

Ghost Dance: A Sequel to Gaston Leroux's The Phantom of the Opera (Historical Mystery/Romance)

Flight Before Christmas (Fantasy Romance, set in the same universe as the Familiar Spirits books)

* Indicates a completed series

About the Author

USA Today bestselling author Christine Pope has been writing stories ever since she commandeered her family's Smith-Corona typewriter back in grade school. Her work includes paranormal romance, cozy paranormal mystery, and urban fantasy, among others. She makes her home in New Mexico.

Christine Pope on the Web:
www.christinepope.com

facebook.com/ChristinePopeAuthor
pinterest.com/ChristineJPope
bookbub.com/authors/christine-pope

www.ingramcontent.com/pod-product-compliance
Lightning Source LLC
Chambersburg PA
CBHW020406260626
47156CB00007B/2251